A Bayou Christmas

A Bayou Christmas

A Louisiana Romance

Susan Sands

A Bayou Christmas
Copyright© 2022 Susan Sands
Tule Publishing First Printing, November 2022

The Tule Publishing, Inc.

ALL RIGHTS RESERVED

First Publication by Tule Publishing 2022

Cover design by Lee Hyat Designs

No part of this book may be used or reproduced in any manner whatsoever without written permission except in the case of brief quotations embodied in critical articles and reviews.

This is a work of fiction. Names, characters, places, and incidents are products of the author's imagination or are used fictitiously. Any resemblance to actual events, locales, organizations, or persons, living or dead, is entirely coincidental.

ISBN: 978-1-958686-32-4

Dear Reader,

So many of you have shown love for this series and I appreciate your support and kindness more than I can say.

Thanks to Tule Publishing for making this hometown series a reality! Thanks to Jane for steering the ship, Sinclair for believing in my work, Meghan for keeping it all running, Nikki for answering my many questions and handling everything you do for authors, and Cyndi for all the book ordering and financials. This is a dynamic, well-oiled machine of amazing people!

Thanks always to Linda Noel, my mom, and first reader of all my books. Christy Hayes, Rosalind Bunn, and Laura Alford, y'all are my tight circle regarding all things books and writing and I don't think I could do it without you. A shout out to the many dedicated reviewers—y'all rock! A special thanks to Mary Brocato from my hometown of Many, Louisiana for promoting my events there and for sharing my book news.

A special thanks to Rennie Clifton, bestie since second grade, for the staunch support and legwork to help get my books into the community where we grew up. You've gone *way* out of your way to help and I love you for it!

This series has truly taken a village to produce and promote!!

Here's to many more!!

All the best,
Susan

CHAPTER ONE

My decade-old SUV started making a strange pinging noise somewhere near El Dorado, Arkansas. It was a gloomy Sunday afternoon and everything I'd passed since Little Rock was locked up tight, so stopping anywhere besides an occasional McDonald's was out of the question. Besides, my car didn't need a side of fries; it needed a mechanic.

If I could just make it the last hundred miles, I planned to sleep for twenty-four hours at least. Well, I would eat first because my exhaustion currently warred with my hunger, and the hunger was keeping me awake right now. This was the farthest I'd ever driven alone and now that my car was getting sketchy, I worked to keep my mind from going to scary breakdown scenarios.

By the time I hit the Louisiana state line, I was gripping the wheel as the sun broke through the clouds. I did *not* want to break down in the middle of nowhere and end up at the mercy of a gun-toting local with a dead animal across his hood. I guessed it was deer-hunting season based on the amount of camouflage I'd spotted when I'd stopped for gas and food after crossing into Arkansas from Missouri.

Come on, come on, come on. I patted the dash of the red SUV I'd dubbed "Big Red" the day I'd driven her off the lot.

She'd seen me through plenty of rough times, so her imminent demise weighed heavily on me. Plus, the cost of buying a new car…that too.

Should I break down, it was a toss-up between calling my new family for help or taking my chances with rednecks in the middle of nowhere. The Bertrands would fly to the rescue in a heartbeat and would probably arrive toting a hot casserole and sweet iced tea in case I was hungry.

My *new* family was my birth family, and we'd met soon after my mom—the one who raised me—died not quite two years ago. I'd gone in search of family roots and found the Bertrands. I'd sprung my existence on them while waiting for a bone marrow transplant to treat the unexpected blood cancer that attacked me while I'd been distracted by my caring for Mom. It was bad enough the Bertrand family had learned about me while I was at my lowest point, and then was made worse when they were forced to care for me for a couple of months after I'd gotten out of the hospital. Well, not exactly forced, but close enough.

If I could just make it a few more miles. "C'mon, girl," I whispered to Big Red. "You can do this."

My luck ran out as I spotted the city limits sign for my destination of Cypress Bayou, Louisiana. Big Red gave up with a rolling sputter and a heavy sigh, and we trundled into a convenience store parking lot. I had mostly made it to my destination. Calling the new family for a rescue felt less cringy since I was now so close.

Before deciding to move here from my lifelong home near Chicago, I'd made a chart with two columns: the plusses and the minuses to determine if I should relocate.

The plusses had won out by only a slight margin.

Sighing over my present predicament, I noticed the auto shop just across the road and thought how great it would be if this had happened on a Monday. I couldn't get cell service where I'd run aground, but I remembered my new sister, Leah, saying it was spotty around town, and sometimes you had to take a few steps one way or the other. And maybe hold your mouth just right. The Bertrands were odd to me, mostly because we were from different cultures, but really, I thought they might just be odd in general for all sorts of other reasons.

I glanced around my car before climbing out, preparing to pace the parking lot with my phone until I got a bar or two on my screen. Thanksgiving was looming and I hoped to get settled before then. Thankfully, the weather was extremely mild compared to Illinois in late fall. The weather went solidly in the plus column of the list I'd used when making up my mind to move here. I loved the year-round green of so many trees and plants here. Chicago pretty much turned brown in September and stayed that way until almost May.

"Hi, there. You got some car trouble?" The deep Southern drawl caused me to nearly jump out of my boots. When I turned around, a tall, dark-haired, dark-skinned man with deep brown eyes and a sprinkling of freckles across his nose stood directly in front of me, smiling.

I nodded, finding my words. "She died just as I pulled in. I'll call my family to pick me up, and I can deal with it tomorrow when things open." I waved a dismissive hand toward the SUV and the handsome stranger. I was parked in a space on the edge of the parking lot, so leaving my car there shouldn't be a problem. This stranger didn't look like danger, but one never knew.

"I work at the auto shop across the street there. I'm happy to help if you'd let me take a look." He pointed over to the shop I'd noticed as I'd rolled to a stop.

He wasn't wearing camo—a plus—though his jeans appeared a little worse for wear with grease stains on them. From what I could tell, his teeth seemed intact, and his long-fingered hands were stained around the nails, which made sense for an auto mechanic, so that checked out. And that smile of his…*wow*.

"I'm Nick Landry." He held out his hand to shake mine. I took it and smiled back somewhat foolishly. I thought he must be Creole, based on some research on the region's history and culture. The town was settled as a French outpost for trade with Mexico in the early seventeen hundreds, which the Spanish controlled at that time. Cypress Bayou was older than New Orleans, and most of the families who lived here had done so for generations.

I must have been staring because he cleared his throat, snapping me out of it. "Thanks for the offer. I wouldn't want to put you out on a Sunday." I wasn't used to anyone stopping to offer help for no reason, but he *did* seem nice.

"No bother. I was working on a carburetor at the shop and ran over here to grab a water." He indicated the bottle in his hand.

There were cars passing at a steady rate, so I wasn't in the middle of nowhere anymore. I exhaled and smiled. "I'd appreciate it." If he was already working in the shop, then maybe at least he could have a quick look.

"Can you pop the hood?"

I climbed back into the car and pulled the release lever for the hood while Nick, the mechanic, lowered his head to have a look.

I could feel a flush creeping up my neck. Had he noticed that I was flustered? I might have to add another item—uh, person—to the plus column on my list: *Nick Landry*.

Now I needed to find some cell service. I got out of the car, leaving the door open and took a few steps in one direction to test my sister Leah's cell service theory. *Sister.* That still seemed like an odd thing to say after growing up as an only adopted child.

But to give Leah credit, she was right. Two bars appeared at the top right of my screen, and I hadn't made any funny faces. I'd call her first since I didn't want to worry my birth mother, Karen, who tended toward the dramatic. Deciding between multiple people to call on was new for me too. It had always been my mom and me after Dad's heart attack.

"Hello?" Leah's voice sounded a little bit like mine, weirdly, but with a Southern intonation. "Allison, is that you?"

I'd stepped away from the car a little farther to keep my conversation private. "Hi, Leah. My car gave up the ghost at the edge of town, but I'm here with a mechanic who's having a look under the hood."

"Oh, no. Tell me where you are, and I'll come get you." She sounded concerned.

"He's still having a look, but I'll call you back if I need a ride. I just wanted to let Karen know I'd made it into town." Karen was a worrywart in overdrive. I'd learned that about her when I was just out of the hospital and weak as a newborn kitten. Nana, my grandmother, had to shoo her away from me regularly because she'd hovered so much.

"Yeah. She's been pacing the floor for the last hour waiting to hear from you, so I'll tell her to sit tight and that you'll be here as soon as possible. Keep me posted and I'll head over and pick you up if the mechanic can't get your car started."

"Thanks a lot." I disconnected the call. That hadn't been too awful.

I moved back toward my car when I ended the call. "Are you new to Cypress Bayou?" Nick asked from his position under my hood.

"Yes. Kind of. I'm moving here from near Chicago."

"Chicago? Well, that's new. I don't know if I've ever met anybody from there."

"Well, I guess you have now." I'd moved closer to where Nick was working to get a better look at my car's nonworking engine. Not that I knew anything about fixing one.

"I hear it's windy." Nick pulled out the dipstick and looked closely at it. I caught the unexpected scent of sandalwood mixed with gasoline.

That made me snort just a little. "Yes. It's windy. And cold. I don't think I'll miss that about it." We made small talk, which was safe and made me more comfortable standing around with a stranger.

"You said you had family in town?" he asked.

"I'm related to the Bertrand family."

He stopped what he was doing and looked at my face. "Oh, I should've guessed it. I can see the resemblance. You're the new daughter." He didn't sound especially surprised by this. "The Bertrands are neighbors of my parents. Known them my whole life. Leah and Carly were a little younger than me, but we grew up pretty close because of our families."

Carly was my new youngest sister, who'd just turned twenty-seven. She was engaged to Tanner Carmichael, who was closer to my age of thirty-five. "I guess that's a bit of a coincidence, huh?"

"Stranger things happen around here all the time, especially lately." He gave a funny eye roll, which made me smile involuntarily.

"If you say so." This small-town thing would take some getting used to. While I'd known my closest neighbors in Naperville, I still ran into strangers there every single day. I had a feeling very few people here didn't know each other.

How I'd ended up here started with my incessant need to know where I came from. Who I'd come from. I'd been burning with questions since I was twelve and found out I was adopted. Turns out, I was the secret baby of the now infamous District Judge Arthur Keller and Karen Bertrand, two lifelong residents of Cypress Bayou.

Of course, the folks here were sparking with questions as soon as I showed up. It was like being the new animal in the zoo that everybody wanted to get a good look at. Even though I'd been the one to seek the family out initially, I admitted my attitude had changed drastically from before.

He snapped the hood shut and said, "I'm sorry to say, we're not going to get your car running today. I'll tow it over to the shop and order your parts."

"How bad is it?" I didn't know if I wanted to hear his assessment, but I got the feeling he was trustworthy.

"Not so bad that you need a new car yet. It's a combustion problem. There's a part that tells the coil when to fire the cylinder, and yours is busted."

Not needing a new car was a good thing right now. "How long until the part comes in?" I felt the heaviness of exhaustion set in after being on the road for so many hours. These days, I only had so much gas in my personal tank.

"Middle of the week if I put a rush on it. Sorry about that."

"Okay. Thanks for your help. I'll call Leah back so she can come and pick me up. Excuse me." I took a couple of steps away to make the call.

"No need. Once I tow it over to the shop, we'll transfer everything into my truck, and I'll take you wherever you're headed in town. Sounds like you've had a long trip already."

"Yes, but that's too much to ask of you. Leah will help me." The man was a stranger offering to give me a ride and move my things. I didn't know whether to worry that he would disappear with me or to fall at his feet in pure gratitude.

"The Bertrands are like family, and my daddy would give me the red ear if I didn't assist a lady in need. Plus, I'm happy to do it. Got nothing else to do on a pretty Sunday afternoon." He looked up to the sky.

I was fairly sure now that he wasn't a serial killer who planned to whisk me away in his white, windowless, serial-killer van. I brought my thoughts back to his comments on the weather. It was crisp and cool, but the sky was cloudless and sunny.

"Thank you, Nick." I couldn't resist asking, "What's the *red ear*?"

He laughed. "My grandma Landry always said that. It means my daddy would fuss at me until my ear turned red if I didn't do right by you."

"Ah, I get it. I've never heard that expression." I'd never heard a lot of expressions that popped out of people's mouths down here. Mostly my family's mouths.

"Yeah. I doubt that's a common one up north where you're from." He shut my hood, pulled out a red bandana that hung from his back pocket, and wiped his hands on it.

"It's the Midwest." I'm not sure why I corrected him. Maybe because he'd dismissed me as a Yankee.

"Pardon?"

"Chicago. It's considered the Midwest, not the North."

"I stand corrected." He inclined his head toward me and my superior knowledge.

I texted Leah to let her know what was happening.

NICK TRIED NOT to stare at Allison. The resemblance was striking to both her sisters, even though the two didn't really look alike. Allison had Leah's facial structure, but she had Carly's shiny dark hair, though it was still a pixie length, and the same facial expressions as Carly when she spoke. She seemed a little pale now, but he knew she'd been very sick only months ago.

Nick infrequently ran into the Bertrands around town

these days because work kept him busy, so it had been a little while since he'd seen them. Nick Landry didn't consider himself a gossip, but his dad referred to his mom as a *nosy neighbor* in jest. But Mom really was a very nosy neighbor. "Sit tight, and I'll go and get my tow truck."

"Thanks." She climbed back into her vehicle to wait.

Nick returned in a couple of minutes driving a flatbed tow truck painted bright blue and yellow. It took him only a few minutes to lift her inert car onto the back. When he was finished, he opened the passenger door and motioned for her to climb inside. Nick efficiently lowered the car into a parking spot behind the building once they'd crossed the street to where the garage was.

"Is that everything?" he asked as they transferred the last few items from her car to his truck. He was glad he'd splurged and gotten the sliding cover for the bed of his pickup, so none of her things would blow out or get damaged.

"I think so." According to his mom, Allison was the eldest of the three Bertrand siblings, taking over that role from Leah now that she'd entered the family.

"Your resemblance to Leah and Carly is striking, but I guess you knew that." Nick made conversation after she'd climbed into his truck as a passenger. He felt like he knew her, even though they'd just met. She seemed so familiar.

"Yes, it's strange when I see them. It's like catching a glimpse of myself in the mirror, but not really."

"So, where are you staying?" He assumed she would be moving in with her nana Elise or Karen, her mother.

She fished out a piece of paper where she'd written the

address and handed it over to him.

Nick looked at the address. "Oh, that's Jake Carmichael's old place. It's a cool loft, right downtown."

"I guess you know a lot about the Bertrands—and the Kellers, huh?" She met his gaze.

He shrugged a shoulder. "Things get around in a town this size. And my mom doesn't miss a chance to fill me in."

"Your mom and Karen seem to have a lot in common—no offense." A smile quirked Allison's lips as she said it. Her mother, Karen, was legend for inserting herself slap in the middle of things going on in town, much like his mom. But he wouldn't say anything ill of Karen to her new daughter.

"Yes, they've known each other most of their lives. And none taken."

"I'm guessing everybody in town knows my story? My family's story." He caught her eye roll and it made him grin.

"Uh-huh. Sorry, but you're walking into the tail end of all the commotion around here with Judge Keller." District Judge Arthur Keller, Allison's birth father, had recently been involved in unsavory behavior. It was to be determined if he would serve prison time or just be stripped of his spot on the bench, politics around here being what they were.

"I expect to be pointed at and whispered about until this dies down. If it ever does."

"The Yankee accent could be an issue," he teased.

She laughed then. "Again, Midwest. But I'll practice my *y'alls* and *bless your hearts* and see how that goes."

It was nice that she had a sense of humor about it all. "You look like you've recovered from cancer well."

She turned to him. "Yes, not being completely bald anymore is nice." She ran a hand through her shiny, dark cropped hair. "I'm ready for it to grow out again."

"It suits you." Her face flushed at his compliment, but he pretended not to notice.

"Thanks."

"Have you seen the apartment yet?" he asked, turning onto Front Street. "You've got a great spot on the river to see the fireworks during Christmas Festival."

"I haven't seen it yet. The family decided where to put me for now."

"You could do a lot worse as far as family, but I guess being new to everyone is a bit daunting."

The fact that he used the word *daunting* made her grin. "Yes, just a bit."

CHAPTER TWO

"Wow, this is gorgeous." I looked around as Nick rolled into a parallel parking space alongside what people here referred to as *the bayou*, which was actually a slow-moving, spring-fed oxbow lake, I'd learned through my town research. This section of downtown Cypress Bayou was charming, and it gave me a little peace getting a glimpse of where I would call home for the next year.

Old bricks paved the street, and iron benches were spaced evenly alongside the water across from the historic section of well-preserved buildings.

"You've not seen the town yet?" Nick appeared surprised at that. "I just assumed you had."

"Last year, I stayed with Nana for a little while after my bone marrow transplant, but the doctors didn't allow me to go out into public spaces because of my compromised immune system."

"Ah. Again, glad you're better."

We climbed out of his truck, and Nick pointed to a New Orleans-esque balcony with scrolled ironwork. "The apartment is upstairs over the old soap store."

I followed his gaze toward the storefront and let my eyes wander up to the scrolled iron balcony. "Wow." The looking up and then looking back down made me a little woozy. I'd been careful not to push myself, but this trip had zapped my energy.

Nick gently steadied me with a hand on my shoulders. "Are you okay? You look kind of pale."

"Maybe a little hungry. And I've had a long couple of days."

Nick shrugged. "Don't pick up anything heavy. I can handle this." He carefully pulled a smallish wooden antique vanity from the truck that I'd not been able to part with. "This is pretty."

"It belonged to my grandmother. It's one of the few things I kept from my mom's house after she died." I'd left the piece uncovered except for a couple of towels to keep it from bumping into something else and getting scratched since I was personally driving things here instead of using a moving company.

"I'm sorry about your mom, Allison." He said it with such touching sincerity that I teared up.

"Thanks. I still struggle with losing her." I cleared my throat, trying to shake loose the clogged sensation. My mom had been my closest friend, especially the last couple of years that she'd been sick. I'd tried so hard to show her how much she meant to me. I'd not exactly been the easiest tween and teen growing up.

"Cypress Bayou will be a big change, huh?" he said, changing the subject, a smile quirking his lips.

"You could say that." I glanced over at the dark water, appreciating its moodiness.

"Be patient with us Southerners. We take a little getting used to."

"I'll do my best. But you get a pass for rescuing me on a Sunday." I really did appreciate his help.

"Don't mention it. It's part of that neighborly thing we do here."

Leah, Karen, and Bob emerged from inside the metal gate that divided the sidewalk from the stairwell leading up to the loft, startling me a little. I hadn't expected them to pop out like that, but given that they'd not let me down yet, it shouldn't surprise me. "Oh, hi. Thanks for coming to meet me."

"I'm so glad you made it. I've been waiting to hear from you *all* day." Karen clutched her hands at her breast like an actress in an old movie. She hadn't changed since the last time I'd seen her. Another thing that would take some getting used to.

"Sorry. I got a late start yesterday. I thought I might be able to make up some time, but there was a ton of road construction." I'd stopped last night for a couple of hours' sleep at an inexpensive motel just off the interstate near St. Louis to break up the almost fourteen-hour drive. "Then my car started acting up a hundred miles or so away. Thankfully, Nick took pity on me where it died and gave me a hand."

They all turned to Nick. "Hey, everybody." He gave a wave. "It's been a while."

"Hey, Nick. Thanks for scooping up our girl and bringing her to us." Bob, Karen's husband, also Leah and Carly's dad, said this.

"Y'all are so welcome, sir. I couldn't leave her stranded, right?" He glanced over at me and grinned. My stomach growled.

"Well, we're thrilled you found her," Karen said and then turned to me. "You know Nick is like family."

"He told me he grew up nearby." Where I was from, we rarely referred to anybody unrelated as family, but I smiled instead of saying so.

"Well, honey, we're glad you're here with us safe and sound." Bob stepped forward to pull me into a big bear hug. I didn't try to avoid it, but it surprised me every time somebody hugged me out of the clear blue.

"Thanks, Bob." Bob had accepted me as a daughter from the first minute I'd met him, which said a lot for a man who'd been kept in the dark by Karen about my existence for thirty-five years. He was a kind, fatherly type who'd slipped past my high wall of defense, reminding me of my dad, who'd been gone for so many years.

Karen placed her hands on each side of my face and simply stared at me with tenderness in her gaze. "Oh, I'm glad you've finally arrived. I was so worried about you driving all that way alone." She hugged me then, and I returned her embrace. When she pulled back, she said, "We'll need to get you to the church so you can meet Father Felix." Her words were like a sudden scratch on a vinyl record that had been playing lovely music.

I stared at her. Surely meeting the priest wasn't part of the deal. "I-uh—"

Leah leveled a steady gaze at our mother. "I think that can wait. Allison's got enough to do with moving here and getting her bearings." Leah put an arm around my shoulders and guided me out of the circle on the sidewalk.

I mouthed a quick "thank you" to her. She grinned at

me, showing an identical dimple to mine. It was so weird seeing my face a few years younger. "Now, let's get your things moved in." They moved as a group toward Nick's truck, everybody grabbing a bag, a box, or some other loose items I'd thrown in the car at the last minute.

I thought about the home I'd left to come here and start a new life—the place I'd lived my entire life until now. I couldn't afford to keep the house on the possibility that things didn't work out here with my new family, so I'd been forced to trust my ever-changing list of pros and cons. Selling my home was a big deal and I'd questioned my decision every day since.

"I had no idea this section of town was so lovely." I looked around, taking in the charming area.

"Jake's rented this loft for *years*," Leah said. "Mrs. Sibley has given him a fantastic deal on the rent as long as he continues to mow her grass and trim the weeds in her yard, though she can well afford to hire someone."

"It's a perfect location. Thanks so much for keeping it available for me." Their kindness at learning of my existence still shocked me. They'd smoothly flipped my long-standing angst toward my unknown family into confused appreciation. I'd been a happy, only child, content in my parents' cozy house with all the love and support a girl needed. Then, when my dad had died right after my twelfth birthday, my mom told me the thing that would forever change me. Shape me. Finding out I was adopted was the worst thing that had ever happened to me, and oh, how I'd struggled knowing someone thought so little of me as to give me away to strangers.

"We only moved out a few weeks ago, so the place didn't sit empty for long. We'll do a housewarming for you during Christmas Festival. You'll have the best view of the lights and fireworks here on the balcony. Jake's always hosted an open house for Christmas Festival."

I guess having a big family was like this—where everybody assumed they were welcome to come over and hang out at your house. "Nick mentioned the festival to me. When is it, exactly?"

"It's the first weekend in December, so we've got a few weeks to get you settled," Leah said. December wasn't far away. I'd come back for a brief visit and Karen and Bob's wedding vow renewal in June when I'd still been wearing a surgical mask outside my home. One of my sisters suggested that Karen had concocted the idea of a vow renewal just to get me to come back here so she could "lay eyes on me."

Once I'd decided to come here, I wanted to arrive before the holidays, so I wasn't alone for Thanksgiving and Christmas. I'd struggled with my recovery these past months, mostly alone. My ex-boyfriend, Hank, hadn't been especially helpful, and he got frustrated that I wasn't getting better as quickly as he believed I should. I had a few friends still in town who'd helped with some heavier lifting like laundry and cooking, but people had their own lives.

The windows of the shuttered business beneath my apartment were covered with brown butcher paper, but the scripted logo *The Soapery* was still splashed across the plate glass. "So, what happened with this place?" I pointed to it as an unexpected pang of sadness filtered through me. A small business failing seemed like such a misfortune.

"Yes, it's a tragedy it shut down." Leah frowned as she stood beside me, staring at the blacked-out windows. "They had the *best* soaps and candles. All the soaps were handmade. I swear you can still smell it in the loft."

"Are y'all ready to head up? This stuff is heavy." Karen carried a small lamp in one hand and the shade in the other.

"Follow me, everyone. Watch your step." Bob led the way up the iron staircase, our feet causing a ringing vibration.

The second I stepped inside the loft, with its airy ceilings, huge windows, and cozy sitting area, I felt like I'd arrived home—well, almost. "Wow." I stood looking all around me. There was a crème-colored sectional; dark-stained end tables; large, navy lamps with barrel-shaped shades; and long, sheer curtains framed the enormous windows. Leah had told me a few weeks ago that the place would be furnished, so I sold most of my belongings instead of moving a house full of furniture. "Who does the furniture belong to?"

"It's yours if you want it. Jake and I bought new stuff for the house. We knew you weren't moving many of your things."

"Thank you." I was an interior decorator by trade, so I began to imagine what I would do here once I found a job. A few splashes of color here and there…

Leah read my mind. "Feel free to make any changes. It's your place as long as you want it. Mrs. Sibley reassured us that she has no intention of selling or raising the rent."

"I'll need to get her information so I can pay her. I don't think I'm quite up to mowing her lawn yet, but—"

"Nonsense. Jake will mow the grass, just like always." Leah waved away my comment.

I did wonder how much the rent was. I was okay for a while, money-wise, thanks to the sale of my mom's house, and because real estate values had increased tremendously since my parents bought the home when I was a baby. Naperville was now a trendy city and close enough to commute to Chicago.

My new nana had plenty of money and strongly believed I deserved some of it for being given away at birth, as she was settling a trust fund on me. Money with strings. The strings being that I had to live here for a year and give us all a chance to get to know each other. Yes, it was extortion, but Nana had helped me so much already.

"Don't worry about the rent until you get on your feet. It's paid up through the end of the year," Leah said. "Oh, and Carly said she would stop by tomorrow."

"I appreciate it, Leah." I didn't know what else to say. These people were so willing to put themselves out for me.

Everyone found a spot to put down the items in their hands.

"I stocked your fridge with a few essentials until you can get to the grocery for what you want. There's bread in the pantry, along with some paper products," Karen said. "You're not gluten-free, are you?"

I shook my head, taken aback at her generosity. "How thoughtful."

"There's soap and shampoo in the master bath. Oh, and I left you a few decent bottles of wine and some beers in the fridge. There's no way we could expect you to come here to be near our family without alcohol." No one denied this. "Oh, and the Wi-Fi username and password are taped to the inside of the pantry door. It's long and random, so I won't try to pretend I know it by heart."

"Of course, we're here for you, dear. Please let us know if there's anything else you need." Bob said this. "I've got some winter squash coming in soon, so stop by the house and grab some."

"Sounds delicious, Bob. I can't thank everyone enough for all your help." Gushing wasn't usually my thing, but gosh, they'd been so nice and thought of everything I might need.

"Nonsense. It's what we do for each other," Leah said.

I gave her a look of pure appreciation. I was touched as I looked around and took it all in. "You're a lifesaver." This was a cliché but so true both literally and figuratively.

"We're thrilled you're here." I appreciated the genuine warmth in Leah's words.

I caught a whiff of gardenias and asked, "So, who owns the retail space beneath the apartment?"

Leah answered, "Mrs. Sibley owns pretty much the whole block. The proprietors of *The Soapery* left shortly after a small fire."

"What a shame."

Nick spoke to me then. "Well, I'd better get going. I'll give you a call when the part for your car comes in."

I recentered my attention toward Nick, who'd stood in the background while I'd interacted with my family. "Thanks again, Nick."

"No problem. It was nice to finally meet you, Allison.

Get some rest, okay?" He then turned to the group. "Bye, everyone."

"Bye, Nick," they said in unison. And there was a repeat of thanks for his kindness.

"Okay, we're gonna clear out of here and give you some peace and quiet. Nana is cooking a big family dinner tomorrow night to celebrate your arrival. Since you don't have a car, someone will pick you up around six o'clock."

"She doesn't have to do that. I don't want anyone to go to any more trouble on my account."

They all laughed at that. Karen stepped toward me and took my hand. "Honey, you're here with your family now, so get used to being helped and fed."

I tried to smile, but it was a struggle. It was all a lot. But since they had taken time and effort to get me settled in my new home, I said, "Thanks again. I'll see you all tomorrow night at dinner."

When the family left, I plopped down on my pristine secondhand sofa and peered at my surroundings, again appreciating the wide-open space and high ceilings. And the light. There was so much light, even this late in the evening.

I might've closed my eyes in pure exhaustion because I woke with a start in darkness, streetlamps providing the only light through the windows. I managed to find the switch on the lamp beside me and click it on.

I hadn't yet been inside the master bedroom, so I turned on lights as I moved through my charming new home, planning on where I would place my small, personal items as I went.

The master bedroom was just as delightful as the rest.

There was a four-poster king-sized bed layered with bedding of neutral and shades of gray, with lots of accent pillows of every texture and size. My designer's heart appreciated the artistry of the place and the décor. It was like a canvas ready for me to add the small touches to make it my own.

The sheets were crisp and appeared new. The thread count was on the high end, so I owed somebody money for their purchases on my behalf.

I went back to the kitchen, realizing that it had been hours since I'd eaten anything. There were all the necessities for a good omelet or a sandwich, but then I noticed the casserole dish with a note on top that read: *So glad you've joined us, darlin'. I hope you like chicken and dumplings.* Nana. Of course.

Nana was the matriarch of the family. She'd taken me into her home when I'd gotten out of the hospital. I was weak and vulnerable, and barely able to walk from one room to the next. She'd put the glow back into my cheeks by feeding me and doing my laundry, and just taking care of me. It had hit me then just how much I missed my mom, but I was glad she'd not lived to see me so sick. That would've been tough for her to take.

Blood cancer was no joke, and neither was the bone marrow transplant with all its chemo and radiation. I was finally feeling almost like myself again, besides the short hair and ten-pound weight loss. Though pans of chicken 'n' dumplings would take care of that if I wasn't careful.

I was starving, so I served myself a very large portion in one of the cereal bowls Leah had left in the cupboard. The aroma of this labor of love filled my nostrils and surrounded me like a warm hug after such an exhausting day of driving.

After eating, I rolled the large suitcase with my weeks' worth of clothes and toiletries into the master bedroom and grabbed the things I would need for the night. The enormous clawfoot tub beckoned me to fill it with hot water and the scented bubble bath sitting beside it. Leah hadn't missed a thing. I could feel a tug of kinship with this middle sister. I'd never had a sister before. Now, I had three counting Elizabeth on my father's side.

I filled the tub and stepped into the steaming fragrant water, still thinking about my new sisters.

Which switched my thoughts to the other side of the family. Things weren't quite as comfortable on that branch of the new family tree, to say the least. My third half-sister, Elizabeth—on my father's side—was a heart surgeon here in town, but she came without the warm fuzzies of the Bertrand girls. She'd been angry and resentful at her father for his secrecy, and I got the impression Elizabeth liked being an only child very much.

Elizabeth had reached out to me when we'd met initially last summer, basically acknowledging that I existed and letting me know not to expect much from them as far as a family welcome. Elizabeth clearly didn't like the Bertrand family and didn't bother to hide that fact.

I'd decided that I was better off without having expectations from my new father and other new sister, or his family. I had enough on my hands with my mother's side of the family—with my mother, Karen, herself. I hadn't completely figured her out yet. She was hugely religious, dramatic, and often passive-aggressive, except during the rare moments, like today, that she allowed her guard down, when I could see and sense her kindness.

I believed Karen when she'd explained that she'd been in dire straits at sixteen and become pregnant by a local guy from a political family. That he'd threatened her with outright denial if she outed his *mistake*, since nobody had seen them together in public. And that giving me up to a loving family seemed like the only way to prevent an end to her future as she'd known it and to make sure I had two parents to love me.

I'd *had* that. Wonderful adoptive parents who'd done everything in their power to raise me well. So, I couldn't blame her for that. Well, except for not choosing me over a well-ordered life that my sisters were privileged to have a couple of years down the road.

My anger came in spurts still. I was exceptionally protective of the little girl I'd been who'd changed so dramatically upon finding out that my birth mother had marked the "no contact" box on the adoption form, which meant she wanted nothing to do with me ever again.

I knew the Bertrands didn't feel that way about me now, though, so that was something.

When I'd found out about my adoption, I became withdrawn and distrustful after I'd discovered that everything I knew was a lie. I wish I could go back now and reassure that little girl. And I wish I could take back all the hateful things I'd said to my mother after she told me. I took it out on her because there was nobody else. I stopped hanging out with friends, afraid they would share new, terrible secrets. I trusted no one.

I knew that Mom worried about what might happen to me when she was gone, hating the idea that I didn't have a lot of friends, and no family left. So a couple years before she died, Mom made me promise to try and find my birth family. I made the promise and didn't follow through until she was gone.

So, here we were. I couldn't change the past and neither could Karen. I would need to decide who I wanted to be—and where I wanted to live after this coming year. Those were my initial goals, at least. I was still in the process of assimilating my faceless family with who they'd turned out to be. I'd created a mental story for so many years that they must be horrible people. But they weren't, even though Karen and Nana's decision to dispose of me as an infant still felt pretty horrible at times. Integrating my past with my present felt pretty daunting to me right now.

CHAPTER THREE

I WOKE UP early, the sun streaming through the windows. Startled at how deeply I'd slept, I pulled on my robe and moved to the window to have a look outside beyond the narrow balcony. The building was very old, and it felt solid, but I'd need to be sure that exterior balcony was safe as well. I figured Leah would know since she'd lived here with Jake over the past year.

There was a steady bustle of people walking on the sidewalk along the bayou or driving by. Some scaffolding had been set up on the grassy area across the water, and a group was working to erect a huge star on the bank of the bayou. I put my face against the window so I could see better.

Then, it occurred to me: the Christmas Festival would happen the first week of December in the downtown area. I'd done some reading about the town and the festival online before I left Illinois. Apparently, this artful display of colorful Christmas lights and large lit set pieces had been growing each year since the early nineteen hundreds until present day.

Instead of sitting around worrying about the unknown, I found the Wi-Fi info and pulled out my laptop and did some deep-dive research on the town and surrounding areas to help quell the anxiety of leaving my hometown and everything familiar. Learning new things was how I'd gotten through some of my roughest times. I watched YouTube videos regularly on how to make and do new things.

As I watched the progress across the water out my window, I heard my phone vibrate. I'd plugged it in to recharge overnight. I grabbed it before it stopped ringing. "Hello?"

"Hi, Allison, it's Nick from the garage. I hope you had a good first night in your new place." His husky drawl caused a sudden thrill to shoot through me. I hadn't had a serious relationship since college, and that was years ago. So, meeting Nick the way I had was—unexpected.

"O-oh, hi. Yes, I slept great." Which was unusual for me since Mom died and through my illness. "Thanks for checking in."

"Glad to hear it. I wanted to let you know that I've ordered the part for your car, and it should be in in two or three business days. So, I'm thinking your car will be ready Thursday or Friday."

"Thanks for letting me know, and thanks again for all your help yesterday." She could picture his smile as he spoke.

"Hey, don't mention it. It was a pleasure to meet you. Let me know if I can do anything for you or even show you around."

I controlled the butterflies at his suggestion of being my tour guide. "I'll keep that in mind. Looks like they're putting up a giant metal star across the bayou this morning." I said this as I continued to watch the workers.

"Yes, it's time for the lit pieces to go up along the bank. There are about two hundred different ones from over a hundred artists, and they'll be covered with lights. You'll be amazed how this place is going to change in the coming days.

The only thing keeping us from living in a Christmas snow globe is the snow. There's no other place as Christmassy as Cypress Bayou."

"Sounds like I moved in at just the right time." The idea of celebrating Thanksgiving with a big, loud family, and living among famous amounts of Christmas lights almost made me smile, but it also threw me back to my childhood memories with my parents, which continued to plague me with sadness since Mom died just shy of two years ago. She'd passed not long before the cancer took over my body, leaving me little time to grieve before survival became my sole focus.

"For sure. Your first Christmas Festival isn't something you'll soon forget."

I guessed he was probably right about that. "I'll look forward to hearing from you once the car is finished. Thanks again."

"Will do. Take care. And let me know if you want a tour guide." There was a question in his tone.

"Thanks, Nick." I disconnected the call and wondered more about him. Did he have a girlfriend? Where did he live? I assumed he wasn't married since he offered to show me around town. And I'd seen the spark of interest in his eyes, despite my still somewhat-pitiful state.

As unsettled as I was, I had no business going out with Nick, or anyone. I needed to focus inward. I'd never felt so unmoored in life as I did right now.

I got a text from Nana then. *Hi darlin'. I hope you're settling in. Sorry I wasn't there yesterday when you arrived. I had a commitment I couldn't get out of. Looking forward to seeing you at dinner later.* ☺

I replied: *Your chicken and dumplings were amazing, Nana. Thanks for doing dinner tonight. See you then!*

Nana and I'd had a special connection from the first day we'd met. She was one of those rare people with whom I'd bonded immediately. She'd said she'd loved me the instant we met, which I soaked in, knowing it must be true. My loneliness had caught up with me and Nana was exactly who I'd needed during my illness.

I showered quickly and dressed, eager to unpack my things and start to make this place my own. I missed my home where I grew up, but it wasn't the same living there alone. Selling my childhood home had been almost as hard as losing Mom. Almost. I'd decided to sell the house once I was solidly back on my feet after I was deemed cancer free by the doctors. Which meant I was not going to die on the heels of Mom's demise. Finding the Bertrands had been timely for me. They'd given me family structure when I'd had no one.

Now, I had hope, something I'd lacked during my two-year ordeal. The idea of an unwritten future kept me moving forward in this new town with my new family, above a defunct soap store.

The fragrances that wafted from below fascinated me. I'd love to get a look downstairs…just to see. My love of all things interior design and DIY had me curious. I had a great respect for anyone who created a thriving business, since that had always been my dream.

The sudden loud buzzing caused me to jump. It took me a second to realize it must be connected to the exterior door. Sure enough, beside the front door, there was an intercom and a button. I pressed it and spoke. "Hello?"

"Hi, Allison, it's me, Carly. I wanted to stop by since I was working yesterday when you arrived."

"Oh, sure." I opened my front door to see my youngest sister with the same hair and smile as me. Well, when mine was long. "Hi there. I'm glad to see you."

We hugged, because that's what these people did, if a little awkwardly on my part—maybe hers too. She wasn't quite as soft, personality-wise as Leah, but Carly was a straight shooter and I appreciated that about her. "Welcome to Cypress Bayou. Just in time for the holidays." Then, she raised her nose to sniff the air. "Yep, I can still smell the honey and lavender from downstairs," she said, referring to the former soap store below.

"Yes. It's pretty distracting—in a good way, I guess."

"We always envied Jake's place, for the smell and the view." Carly moved to the large window and looked outside. "It's starting already. People are putting up lights." She pointed to the bank across the water.

"Yes, I noticed the huge star."

"I'm thrilled you arrived in time to see it all."

"I'm excited for my front-row seat. So where do you and Tanner live now?" I asked, knowing they were currently building a house nearby, but also that it wasn't yet finished.

Carly laughed out loud. "We're living in Tanner's Airstream trailer that's parked on our property along the bayou."

"Uh, wow. Isn't that kind of small?" I envisioned a tiny travel trailer like I'd seen on TV.

"*So* small. But it's okay for now, I guess. We work together at the law office, so there's a bigger space to escape to every day. Plus, it will make me appreciate having a house of my own that much more."

"You should have moved in here. I could've lived in the trailer." That made so much more sense to me.

Carly waved a hand to dismiss my concerns over her lack of space. "Tanner likes his trailer, believe it or not. And I've gotten used to it. Our house will be done in a few weeks, so we'll stick it out until then. I'm glad you were able to move in here." According to my sisters, Jake and Tanner's grandfather had left them some acreage that had been in their mom's family for ages. The land was at the south end of Cypress Bayou. The family land was where both my sisters would live.

Last summer, Tanner had offered Carly a job at his new firm after she'd graduated from law school and moved back to town. They'd been instrumental in the takedown of Tanner and Jake's father, Carson Carmichael, and Allison's own birth father, Judge Arthur Keller, for all means of law-breaking bad behavior.

I hadn't heard the entire list of things our fathers had been charged with but from what I'd gotten, their corruption over the years had affected a large percentage of the residents in Cypress Bayou in some way. So, one of my sisters helped put my other sister, Elizabeth's father—and mine—in jail, though the judge was currently out on bail. I'm sure I would get a fuller accounting of the story over time.

"I love this place; I've got to admit." I scanned the room again.

"Well, enjoy the quiet for a little longer. Things are ramping up for the holiday season. Everything from here on will be jingle bells, Christmas lights, and hot cocoa until the first of the year."

"I don't think that'll be such a bad thing. It's going to be a huge improvement over last year." I nearly shuddered at the thought of Christmases the past couple years while Mom was so sick, and then right after her death. I could only hope for distraction this year.

"I'm so sorry about your mom, Allison. Momma can be a real piece of work, but I can't imagine not having her around." They'd all been lovely and kind about my mom's passing.

"Thanks, Carly."

"And welcome again to our wacky family. It will likely be an exercise in patience for you, but everybody means well." Carly grinned at me, and I had that mirror sensation again. She was nearly a decade younger than me, and a reminder of how I'd aged in that time. Besides the usual fine lines, my soul had aged. I was no longer that fresh, dewy young woman like I'd been in my twenties.

I shrugged a shoulder. "It's intimidating, I admit. I'm not used to so many people asking about my personal life. I'm a pretty private person, boring even, so I'm surprised when it happens."

She laughed. "Well, boring you're not, and I'm sorry to say that privacy is a luxury you won't find much within our family or here in Cypress Bayou. Someone will always try and wring any secrets right out of you when you attempt to keep anything on the down low, or even any details to yourself—about anything."

Her words made me want to shudder, so instead I asked,

"Sounds like tonight will be a feast, huh?"

"You know Nana well enough to understand her need to celebrate your homecoming with a large family meal."

She was right about that. "There were chicken and dumplings in my fridge from her when I arrived yesterday."

"Of course. Never a shortage of comfort foods around here. And you now live within a minute of the best restaurants in the area."

"Yes. I might go out later and walk around to get a little exercise and see the downtown. When I was here the first time, I was too sick, and later I was so busy with Karen and Bob's vow renewal ceremony." And I'd still been sick and not able to get out much. But Karen had insisted I come to town for their event.

"Yeah. That wasn't cool of Momma to extort you to travel back here for her ceremony when you were just beginning to recover. She was determined to see you again, and she's nearly unstoppable when she gets a bee in her bonnet like that."

"I did okay. But being bald in a purple dress wasn't the best look for me. I hope she doesn't have those photos displayed anywhere people can see them."

Carly laughed at that. "Those purple dresses weren't flattering on any of us."

"I think she called them lavender, but I'm pretty sure they were beyond lavender."

"Oh, there's no doubt we looked like a bunch of grapes that sat too long on the vine."

I snickered. "I'm glad I'm not the only one who thought so." Leah and Carly had made cracks about their dresses throughout the time I'd been here, which had gotten on Karen's nerves. But a lot of what people said and did got on Karen's nerves.

"Tanner and I can swing by and pick you up this evening if that's okay. Leah told me about your car trouble. I'm glad Nick was able to help. He's a great guy."

They discussed Nick as if he were part of their family and a trusted friend. "Yes, I'm relieved he's taking care of it for me. He was so kind to haul my stuff over here on a Sunday."

"I'm not surprised. He takes care of all our cars and services them. Plus, I've known him my entire life."

"So, I guess I'll plan to see you later. Around six?"

CHAPTER FOUR

Tanner and Carly picked me up as promised. I'd only met Tanner briefly during my visits to Cypress Bayou and had forgotten what a big, handsome man he was. His brother, Jake, had been key to my medical care once I'd had the transplant and was released to his care in Cypress Bayou, so I'd gotten to know him pretty well, considering. Jake was a doctor at Cypress General in town.

Tanner and Jake only recently discovered they had a half-sister named Lisa, who'd also gone on a journey to find her birth family. Her search led her to uncover some dark truths she'd not known about her family. I felt a kinship with Lisa, whom I'd met last summer when I was in town. I wondered how common it was to discover an unexpected sibling. So far, there were two in the Bertrands' extended family. Maybe it was something about this place.

Nana's house sat on a small hill at the end of a long drive, with a view of the bayou behind it. Like a set in a movie. It was a bygone remnant from Civil War days. Think *Gone with the Wind*. The historic property had been passed through the family for a hundred years, at least. And Nana considered it her sacred duty to maintain the home and property to a high shine. Not that it wasn't comfortable or homey, because it was. In fact, it was the hub of the family for important and unimportant meetings, dinners, and parties.

The first time I'd seen *Plaisance House*, I was stunned by its beauty. Then, when I'd had the opportunity to live in it for just over a month to recover, I'd felt like a princess in a fairy tale. So, coming back here brought back a recent pleasant memory.

Nana met us at the door and pulled me in for a tight hug, one that belied her size. She was still a strong woman, despite her age. "Oh, I'm so happy you're here, darlin'."

"Hi, Nana. It's great to see you. I'm glad to finally get settled and have that drive behind me."

"Well, let's get you inside so we can catch up." She led the way through the foyer, with its sky-high ceiling and huge crystal chandelier.

I noticed the scent of beeswax combined with the rich, spicy aroma of something cooking. "It smells amazing, Nana. What are you cooking?" I'd unpacked boxes and bags all afternoon, only stopping to make a quick sandwich for lunch just before noon. I was famished.

"I've made a pot of red beans and sausage and enough stuffed crabs to feed my army twice." She turned to me and grinned as we swept through the swinging door that led to the kitchen.

Leah and Jake arrived not five minutes later and were followed in by Bob and Karen. The kitchen got loud very quickly with laughter and the constant sibling jabs that competed only with Karen's occasional snide remarks at how much fun everyone but her seemed to have. Karen was consistent; I'd give her that. She loved being the center of attention, and when she wasn't, she got miffed.

I kind of understood the being left out thing, my adoptee angst aside. Not having history with these people, I'd experienced a little "outsider" syndrome of my own when the entire group was together, or when Carly and Leah exchanged knowing looks. I hated that it bothered me.

Karen cornered me as I sat down at the large kitchen table. "It's good to see you, dear. We never did decide on a time for you to come and meet with Father Felix." She wore a determined expression.

I'd watched my two Bertrand sisters enough to understand that if I gave in to Karen's demands, they would never stop, so I said, "Are you friends with the priest?"

"Of course, dear. I'm at church a *lot*, as you might have heard. And I worry so much for the souls of my girls. You know, Leah and Carly will hardly pass through the doors of our church anymore." And I assumed there was a good reason why.

"I'm not Catholic, Karen. And I'm sorry that I don't have any real interest in meeting with Father Felix." There, I'd said it. I'd stood my ground with my new mother, who regularly manipulated everyone in the family to do the things she wanted.

Karen's face flushed and she opened and closed her mouth like a trout on a line. "B-but I just assumed you'd want to join me at church now that you're here to stay." Zealots never understood that they were zealots, in my experience. I didn't judge her for her need to be part of her church's inner workings, but it wasn't how I'd lived my life. We'd attended church on the usual Protestant holidays:

Easter and Christmas. If I was led at some point to do more, it would be because I wanted it.

I shook my head. "I'm sorry, Karen, but I don't. I realize it's important to you, and if I decide that's what I want at some point, I'll let you know." I said it kindly, but with no doubt I meant it. "But I'd love to get together and do other things."

Karen ignored that last part. "Well, I'm sorry to hear that. I'm so disappointed."

Great. Now, I'd *disappointed* my new mother. I steeled myself against rolling my eyes, which would've been my natural reaction to this nonsense. Maybe she should've considered *her* soul when she marked the box on the adoption papers: *no contact*. I still had an unexpected nasty thought or two about my adoption circumstances, and it's possible I always would.

Leah approached and obviously noticed our tension. "Hey there, Allison. What's up?"

I didn't want to relay what had just passed, so I said, "Nothing much."

"She doesn't want to meet Father Felix or go to church with me." Karen pouted like a child when she said it, as if she were telling on me.

I could see the annoyance pass across Leah's expression. "Momma, we discussed this. Church is *your* thing. Being buddies with the priest is *your* thing. Father Felix would tell you not to try and push religion on others in a way that makes them turn around and run the other way."

I didn't respond to that, but I agreed with the statement. This dynamic was pretty upside down. Like the daughters were the mothers and Karen was a naughty child. I imagined growing up with Karen as a mom. There were some things I was glad to have missed not being raised in this family.

"I can't help but hope you will *all* change your minds." Karen's expression was hurt. Possibly it was a contrived hurt. Possibly not. "Someday."

"There are lots of other things we can do together." I reiterated the idea that she'd ignored. "I'd love to get together over coffee or lunch soon." Pretty much anything but dogmatic indoctrination with the padre.

Leah handled Karen a little harshly because Karen didn't do subtlety. She liked for everyone to think how she did and fall in line. It was clear that Leah and Carly both refused to be bullied by their mother. Our mother. I did wonder what it must've been like when Karen had all the power over her children.

The doorbell rang above the din of noise, and Nana immediately left the room to answer it. "Who else is coming?" Karen asked Leah.

"Hmm. Not sure." Leah lifted her shoulder in a shrug.

A wave of pleasure washed over me when Nana swept in holding Nick's hand and leading him inside the kitchen. There was something about that guy.

"I've invited dearest Nick to our celebration dinner for Allison since he was so helpful in bringing her to us when her car broke down." Nana made this announcement as she took advantage of the break in conversation.

"Hi, everyone." Nick lifted a hand in greeting.

He received a warm welcome, but no one reacted with any real surprise over his appearance at a family dinner.

Nick's eyes moved through the room until they found mine. He smiled at me, and I smiled back, likely turning as red as a peeled tomato.

Once again, my breath caught at his smile. It was dynamic and warm. I wondered at how much orthodontia work he'd had done, as his teeth were utterly perfect.

"All right, everyone, come and serve your plates." Nana raised her voice just enough to be heard over the conversations taking place in the room. Again, I marveled at the number of people who'd gathered as family for a simple meal. I got that they were celebrating my return, but this kind of gathering might happen on any given Sunday with the Bertrands. I'd been an only child with only an aunt and uncle and one grandmother as extended family, who'd lived across the country, who were older and now deceased. I barely remembered three of my grandparents, except for my mom's mom, who I'd spent time with as a child.

I moved toward the serving line that was forming when my stomach growled loudly. "How are you settling in?" I nearly jumped at how close Nick was behind me. His warm breath tickled my ear as he spoke. I sensed his body close to mine, but not quite touching as we moved forward in line.

"I'm doing well, thanks. I unpacked all my stuff today, so it's feeling a little more like home." I turned my head when I spoke so he could hear me from behind.

"I'll plan to bring your car over to you when I get it fixed."

His kindness was appreciated, but I didn't want to get accustomed to feeling like I owed him. "I can get someone to drive me over to pick it up. I don't want you to go out of your way again. You've already done too much." And yes, he was very attractive, something I could admit.

"That's completely up to you, but keep in mind that the offer still stands."

They served plates and found seats at the oversized dining table in Nana's kitchen/breakfast area. Nick sat a few seats down from me even though there was an available space beside me. I wondered if he'd taken my words as me not wanting to be so friendly. With the sudden distance between us, I experienced an acute aloneness in this crowd of people whose bonds had been cemented to one another decades ago.

I could feel myself saying all the right things, but my interactions with them sometimes felt a little forced. They made assumptions about who I was—in a good way. Maybe I wasn't as nice as they believed. How could they even know me after such a short time? I didn't want to offend anyone, so I didn't let on that I didn't quite fit in and went with the flow. Fortunately, they weren't an easily offended bunch, besides Karen. She was impossible *not* to offend, unless you did everything she said.

"So, Allison, do you have any ideas on what your next move might be?" Leah asked this from beside me, but she'd said it loudly enough that everyone around the table paused to hear my answer.

"Um, well, I haven't made any decisions yet, but something in interior design. That's my background." Finding a job was my next step, and I'd been thinking a lot about which direction I might go with it. I didn't reveal my heart's desire to run my own shop. It was a tightly held, *maybe someday* kind of dream. I'd been so close to it too before

Mom got sick.

"There are a couple of accessories shops in town that also have design-for-hire options," Nana chimed in as we all continued to eat. "I'll ask around town and see if anyone's hiring."

"Thanks, Nana. I also do industrial design and space planning for businesses, so maybe I'll see what's available in both areas." It was likely going to be hard starting out in such a tight-knit place. Every job I might get potentially took work away from someone else—someone established and local. I'd had that experience in Naperville even, and it was a far larger community than Cypress Bayou.

"Jake works at the hospital with countless doctors and health professionals, Tanner and Carly can spread the word among their clients, and Karen works at the preservation society, where there is always a need for design services as the historical homes need sprucing up." Nana listed how they might help me.

Karen added, "Yes, dear, I can mention you at church and the garden club as well."

I was overwhelmed with the bombardment of offers to help me get on my feet professionally. "Thanks, everyone. I appreciate it."

As much as I was eager to get back to work, I hesitated to accept their kindness. I wondered if my living here was going to even work out, for one thing. How much family overreach could I comfortably live with? Would I ever get used to everyone's well-intentioned nosiness about my life and my decisions?

It was all yet to be determined, so any job I took would

be just that—a job for now.

Thankfully, they moved on to a vibrant discussion on the progress of Bob's winter vegetables in his backyard garden. "The beets and carrots are coming along quite nicely this season, as are the chives and lettuces."

Bob's garden was legend in the area, according to Karen, and he was often asked to speak at the garden club and at the local university due to his *master gardener* status. It was one of the first things I'd learned about him when we'd met. While I recovered at Nana's house and gotten a little stir-crazy, I'd gone over to Karen and Bob's and sat inside his greenhouse while he'd repotted seedlings for the herb garden.

After dinner and a dessert of bread pudding with rum sauce and ice cream, we cleared the dishes, and everyone did their part to return Nana's kitchen to its former clean state. I wiped down the table and gathered the place mats with magnolia blossoms printed on them. I missed the summer smells here: the flowers and warm, humid breezes after the rain. Now, cinnamon and cloves were everywhere, which I loved only slightly less. Maybe I should find the nearest candle store.

"You look a little lost. Everything okay?" Carly asked.

"Yes, I'm fine. Just remembering how wonderful the magnolia blossoms smelled last summer." I held up the place mat in my hand.

Carly smiled. "Yes, I miss the summer when it's gone, but then I miss the winter holidays when it's summer too."

"Is there a candle store in town? I would love to have a few Christmas-scented ones around." Buying candles for the loft might be just the thing I needed. I'd always had them back home and they never failed to brighten my mood. I loved the Fraser fir scent since we'd only had artificial trees through the years. Of course, I always had some kind of smell in the apartment already, but I never know what it might be day to day.

"Well, the soap store under your apartment had the best candles. But you can probably make do with the hand-made ones at the hardware store down the block from where you live. Those are awesome too."

"I'll check it out. Thanks."

"Hey, we're going to head out now. Are you ready to go?" Carly asked.

Before I could answer, Nick spoke from the end of the table. "I can take you home, if you want to stay a little longer."

"Yeah, everybody else will be here awhile. Unless you're tired. We understand that you're not quite back to your old self, so always feel free to speak up if we're too much."

Before thinking it through, I turned to Nick. "I'll take you up on your offer." Nana went to so much trouble on my account with this meal tonight that I should stay another half hour at least. The smart thing to do would be to plead exhaustion and hightail it out of there. I could feel myself wearing down from all the unpacking today, and still from the drive. But obviously I wasn't feeling so smart now, because the idea of cute Nick driving me home gave me a little tingle. Something that hadn't happened in a very long time.

"Okay. Now I don't feel so badly about leaving too soon. We've got court early in the morning." Carly laid a hand on my shoulder. "I'm so glad you've come back to Cypress Bayou, Allison. The whole family is."

"Thanks. I appreciate your saying that." I wanted to feel something besides appreciation for my sisters and my new parents and grandmother. Of course, I did feel love for Nana. Part of the reason for moving back here was to find a sense of family with these almost-strangers, so maybe it was up to me to try a little harder.

"You okay?" Nick asked after Carly left.

I nodded, but didn't reply, only stared toward Carly and Leah embracing. They saw each other several times a week. The hugging thing was a little much.

"Seems like they've pulled you right into the family." Nick's observation made me wonder if he could read minds.

"They are nice people. I just don't know them that well yet." It was true and neutral.

"Makes sense. But I don't remember any of them saying things they don't mean. Just so you know."

I stared at Nick for a second. "I'll keep it in mind."

He frowned then and looked around them. "It's a lot, I'm guessing."

"Yeah. It's a lot."

We were interrupted by Karen, who'd clearly had a couple cocktails, based on her bright eyes and slight slur. I'd been warned to stay clear of her after cocktail hour by my sisters. "My oldest girl. I'm so sorry I gave you up. I wish I'd known that things would work themselves out eventually."

This was such an awkward and uncomfortable conversation to have out in the open. Of course, Karen had said almost the same thing last year. And I'd not said much in response, because what did one say? *Yeah, me too. I wish I'd grown up in this big, close-knit, kind-of-weird family with plenty of money.*

Bob showed up at that moment and rescued me. "Okay, dear. Let's get you home." He offered the sleeves of Karen's coat to her, distracting her from my answer. "Allison, dear, we're glad you've come back." Bob kissed the top of my head and whisked Karen away.

"See how awkward that is?" I motioned toward my birth mother's retreating back.

Nick had witnessed the scene. "Yes, I see what you mean."

"I'm ready to go now." I stood from the table and went to find Nana in the kitchen rearranging the placement of the dishes in the dishwasher. I almost laughed at that. She let everyone help, then went behind us and redid everything.

"Y'all headed out now?" She looked a little tired, which was odd. I didn't remember ever seeing her without her usual sparkle. But I knew she wouldn't want me to mention it in front of Nick, who was standing behind me.

"Nick's driving me home, but I wanted to thank you for hosting such a lovely dinner in my honor."

"Darlin', it was my pleasure." The older woman's eyes crinkled at the corners, and I noticed her getting a little teary. "Don't be a stranger, okay? And don't let Karen bully you. She's my daughter, but I understand how uncomfortable she might make you sometimes."

"I guess she's been through a lot." Truth was, I no longer held quite as much of a grudge against Karen now that I knew her. Nobody could fix the past completely. On the one hand, I could've grown up as Karen Bertrand's eldest daughter. But who knew if she would have ever met Bob in that instance and had Leah and Carly? So, it was silly to romanticize my growing up as their big sister with the whole family surrounding me with comfort and love. It might have been a disaster for all of us.

I'd had comfort and I'd had love, just on a much smaller scale, though I'd always wondered who my birth parents were, and like every other adoptee, why I'd been given away with no option for contact when I was grown.

"So have you, and we all know this hasn't been easy for you. Especially after your illness. Please let me know if there's anything I can do for you while you adjust to this new environment and continue to heal." Nana's kindness pulled me in.

Nana had taken such wonderful care of me, so she understood me a little better than the others. "Thanks, Nana, for understanding." She pulled me into a hug.

CHAPTER FIVE

H E SMELLED LIKE sandalwood tonight, which was one of my very favorite male scents. I had a thing about smells, especially good ones. When I'd been so sick, it was one of the senses I'd lost for several months. Now, I appreciated it even more.

It was full dark and getting cold by the time I climbed into Nick's truck. He hadn't said much this evening, seemingly content to sit back and enjoy the gathering and the food. "Tonight was fun. Nana was kind to include me, even though I'm not part of the family."

"I think Nana wanted you to know how much she appreciated you helping me. I'd had a long couple of days packing up and driving. Before my cancer, it wouldn't have been a big deal, but these days I get overtired and overwhelmed by my weakness." I smiled over at him in the dark. "And it sounds to me like you pretty much are a part of the family."

"I've always considered the Bertrands and Nana family."

We parked alongside the bayou across from my apartment and I noticed that there were some bright white Christmas lights on the giant star I'd watched the workers set up yesterday. "Wow, this is early for the lights, huh?" I asked. When researching the festival online, I noticed the

"Light up the Holidays" event was scheduled right around Thanksgiving, which was just over a week away.

"They test the lights as they put up the big structures. So, some nights you'll see different ones lit up here and there until festival time."

I stared out over the water. "It's so pretty, even with just a couple pieces turned on. I can't imagine how awesome having everything lit up beside the water will be." The lights shone off the water, creating a mirror effect.

"I'll enjoy watching it through your eyes. I've grown up with it every year that I can remember, so I tend to take it for granted. It's fun when somebody is new to the festival."

"Does it ever snow here?" I'd not asked anyone that yet.

He laughed. "Not often, but we do get the occasional snowfall or ice storm. Mostly ice, when it happens, and that's usually in January."

"I keep telling myself I won't miss the snow and the cold, but since it's getting so close to the holidays, I'm not sure now. There's always a good chance of snow for Christmas where I come from."

"I've seen the pictures on TV."

We chatted like old friends sitting there in his pickup. I was comfortable with Nick, which surprised me after what I'd gone through the past two years. "Well, I'd better go inside and get some sleep. I'm planning to dive into job hunting tomorrow."

"I hope you find something. If there's anything I can do to help, let me know. I'll keep my ears open. People talk a lot while waiting to have their cars fixed."

"Hmm. I've never thought about that. I guess sitting

around with nothing else to do but wait might spur people to talk on their phones."

"Around here, people do a lot of talking to each other. And that's where the interesting conversations happen."

"Back home, it would be unusual for me to run into somebody I knew at the car repair shop. Not impossible, but a lot less likely."

"Well, you're not in Chicago anymore, Allison, and here, everybody knows everybody."

It sounded nice for everyone to know you, in theory, but I could already see the downside to that. "Thanks again for the ride home, Nick." I suddenly didn't want to get out of the truck. It was warm and comfortable. And I'd enjoyed our short ride home together, and our chat here in the moonlight. But I wasn't ready to invite him in for a visit in case it sent the wrong signal. I reached for the door handle and pulled it with no luck.

"Wait, hang on. That door sometimes sticks in the cold." Before I could try the handle, he'd jumped out and opened my door for me. He insisted on seeing me safely across the street and to my door.

"Thanks again."

"Anytime, Chicago girl."

The first thing I noticed when I stepped inside the loft was the strong scent of vanilla and cinnamon. That was a new one.

THE NEXT TWO days I spent exploring the immediate area. I

found the nearest grocery store, a few restaurants that appeared promising, and spent a little time going in and out of the closest gift stores and cafés. I bought the local print newspaper and enjoyed going through it with my morning coffee. There weren't many ads that seemed helpful to my job hunting, but I learned that little Mikey LeBlanc killed his first deer. There was a short write-up about how many antler points the deer sported and it showed a photo of the grinning boy holding up the rack.

Back home this wouldn't have qualified as "news". But I had to admit it was entertaining, and something I would have told my mom about.

I shivered as I climbed out of bed Thursday morning, rubbing my arms to take out the chill. The place had been comfortable since my arrival, until today. Now, I searched out the thermostat and turned the unit to "heat".

I made coffee, automatically going over to my window to see what was happening out there this morning. Had it been warmer, I would've sat on my tiny balcony that overlooked the bustling street and the water while I sipped my coffee. I'd been reassured by Jake that the balcony was reliable.

Today, the apartment smelled like jasmine and magnolias. Every time I noticed the scents, it made me wonder just how much scented soap and candles were down there permeating my floorboards.

As I organized a list of job options, the smell became stronger from downstairs. So much so that I was having a hard time concentrating on my lists. I'd gotten the landlord's name and number from Leah, so maybe it was time to give her a call. I dialed the number and an elderly voice answered,

"Hello?"

"Hi, Mrs. Sibley, this is Allison Miers. I've just moved into your lovely apartment on Front Street—"

"Oh, yes, yes. How are you, dear? Are you getting settled? Is there anything you need?" She peppered me with questions.

"I'm doing fine. The apartment is just perfect. I wanted to reach out and thank you for allowing me to move in and to set up my rent payments."

"Well, the rent's paid through the end of December, so we don't have to worry about yet. I'll give you my address so you can drop off a check around the first of the year. Or you can pay ahead if that's easier." Her suggestions made me remember that I needed to open a local bank account.

I hadn't written anyone a check in quite a while now that there was Venmo and PayPal. I took down her address. "Oh, and I wanted to ask about the space downstairs…the old soap store?"

"Well, the nice folks left rather abruptly after the fire. They said there was a family situation, and they were needed back home in Arkansas. I had my handyman go in and fix the damage. He said they'd left an awful lot of stuff in there, but I haven't had the energy to spend time looking around. I figured I'd rent it out again eventually. The soapery did a rather good business from what I could tell."

"Is there any way I could have a look at the place? It's just out of curiosity. I smell some of the loveliest scents that waft up into my apartment." I wasn't even sure why I wanted to see it, honestly, other than the scented soaps.

"Of course, dear. You can pick up a key from my front porch and let yourself in to have a look around."

"Oh, okay. I'd like that. I'll come by around noon if that's all right."

"Lovely."

I quickly showered and dressed in jeans and an oversized sweater. According to my weather app, a cold front had blown through overnight, and the mild temps had dropped about twenty degrees. No wonder I'd had to turn the heat on.

I ate a quick, midmorning breakfast since the coffee was now gone and I'd gotten hungry. I looked over my list then, killing time until I left for Mrs. Sibley's house.

There was a large, higher-end furniture store who advertised design services, an architecture firm in town I thought I'd check in with just in case they needed someone, and a couple of accessories shops on Front Street near my apartment. I hadn't noticed any "help wanted" signs, but we were in the middle of the holiday season and somebody might need temporary employees. Despite the trust fund, I needed to get back out into the world. Plus, the money wasn't mine until I'd been here a full year. I'm certain Nana would help me out if I needed it, but thankfully, I didn't for now.

Mrs. Sibley's house was within walking distance, according to my phone's map, so I grabbed a light jacket to put over my sweater for the walk over. My boots had rubber soles, so they would be good for walking several blocks.

As I exited the side stairs from the loft, I shivered a little in the wind. I headed south on Front Street and crossed over so I could walk along the water's edge in the sunshine.

Decorating was happening in full force everywhere I looked. Crews of men and women who appeared to be volunteers, were gathered in small groups working together. Some were up on ladders and others were feeding them strings of lights to embellish the many large pieces set up since yesterday. Everyone appeared to know exactly what they were doing.

I could sense the community atmosphere everywhere I looked. They were working together but were also talking and laughing. Very few stared at cell phones. It was something I often noticed because my mom had been so against my having one as a teen. She stopped fighting it toward the end of my high school years because it was obviously a losing battle, and things were at the point where "everybody" had one, but I'd remained sensitive to the time I spent on my phone if anyone else was nearby.

I laughed to myself. Maybe I gave this place too much credit. It's possible they didn't use their phones all the time because they couldn't get service.

When I got to the railroad tracks, I turned right. The entrance to the university was dead ahead. One day I would check out the campus. Someone had said it was gorgeous and old, like everything else around here.

Mrs. Sibley's address was one street over from mine, but at the other end. She lived in a largish A-frame home with a sizable front yard. The house was painted a pale yellow and it had a covered front porch with white rockers for sitting. There were several colors of roses still in bloom out front and I wondered what variety they were to still look so fresh. The first frost would likely kill them, which saddened me a little.

I stepped onto her porch and looked around for the

key—or something where the key might be but found nothing. There was a small, metal letter box attached to the house beside the door, so I looked in there, just in case. Empty. So, I rang the doorbell, hoping not to disturb my landlady.

Mrs. Sibley was a tiny woman who used a cane. Her hair was styled, and she was dressed in a pink tracksuit with a white crocheted shawl around her shoulders, which made me smile. "Well, hello there. You must be Allison."

"Yes, hi. I'm sorry to disturb you but I don't see the key out here anywhere."

"Oh, it's here somewhere. Come on in, dear, while I dig around for it."

"I wouldn't want to intrude—" I hesitated to enter her home.

"Nonsense. You won't take all my gold and jewels now, would you?" She gave me a side-eye and a grin.

I laughed, charmed at her sharpness and sense of humor. "I wouldn't know what to do with gold and jewels, ma'am."

Stepping inside, I noticed a surplus of crocheted doilies. There was a doily under every single item that sat on a surface. There were afghans here and there as well. "Did you crochet all of these?" I asked, lightly touching an intricate pattern on the foyer's entry table.

"I've been working my yarn for years, as you can tell." She made a sweeping motion around the room. "I've made many things."

"Wow, that must take a lot of time." I had to admit that I was totally impressed by her skill. When I was very young and my grandmother was still living, she'd tried to teach me to knit. Since I'd failed miserably, she then showed me a basic crochet chain stitch and then how to add rows. It was something I hadn't thought about in years. I recalled several square pot holders I'd made during my crochet phase.

I'd always made crafts of every kind, any DIY project I came across—picture frames, macrame. Having been an only child, I read a lot as well.

"Oh, honey, I've got nothing but time. Do say you'll stay for a cup of tea. It's cold out there today." She'd reached inside a drawer beside one of her two recliners and fished out the key and handed it to me.

I didn't have the heart to grab her keys and decline the tea. "Sure. I'd love to."

I learned that Mrs. Sibley had no children of her own. "But I've got a few nieces and nephews who'd like to get their hands on my house and property when I die."

Not knowing how to respond to that, I asked, "So, you've rented the loft to Jake Carmichael for a long time, I hear."

She grinned, showing a full set of teeth. "That scamp. He's been like a son to me since he was in high school. I hired him to mow my grass every week, and we always shared a lemonade when he was done. And he still does it, you know. When he was out of town doctoring, he sent his big brother, Tanner, to do it. They're good young men, those Carmichael boys." Then, she leaned closer, which invited me to do the same. "But that daddy of theirs is bad news. Always has been if you ask me. I guess you heard what happened a few months back."

"Well, yes, but I've been living in Illinois, so I've only

heard a little from my family here and there." I almost said, "my new family", but now that I was here, I should probably drop the *new*. Fact was, they were my family, new or not.

Mrs. Sibley's brows drew together, she tapped her chin, and then her eyes widened as if she'd just figured something out. "That's right, Arthur Keller is your *daddy*, isn't he? I'll tell you, that was some surprise when it all came out. How's it going with that sister of yours, Elizabeth?" Mrs. Sibley's eyes twinkled at the possibility of learning some scoop about my family. "She's a real pistol, isn't she?"

"I think Elizabeth was shocked when she found out she had a sister." I didn't want to disparage anyone for gossip's sake, even though the elderly woman didn't seem to have bad intentions. I thought maybe she was lonely and keen on the excitement of learning something new.

I got the same strange sensation sitting here with Mrs. Sibley as I had when I'd barely met Nick and he had easily discussed the goings-on involving my family—like he knew me before we'd met.

Before it went any further, I finished the tea in my cup, stood, and said, "Thanks again for the tea and conversation. I'll return the key to your mailbox later this afternoon."

"Oh, dear, have I offended you?" Mrs. Sibley appeared slightly chagrined, and I couldn't tell if she was being cagey or if she was remorseful for making me uncomfortable with all the talk of my family.

"Of course not. I just have a long list of things to do today, so I'll get going."

"All right, dear, come by anytime."

CHAPTER SIX

As soon as I entered the darkened retail space beneath my apartment, I was assailed with a conglomeration of scents. Balsam, eucalyptus, coconut, lavender…so many that I couldn't identify them all. Some people could identify everything in a cooked dish when they tasted it. I, on the other hand, could sniff the air and identify smells. After several years in the design business, I could tell jasmine from magnolia.

I found the light switch on the wall and flipped it. The lights came on, which surprised me a little, seeing how the storefront was currently unoccupied. I noticed that there were wooden shelves against the walls and round tables set here and there, for displays, I assumed. I hadn't told anyone I was going to be in here, probably because I couldn't give a good excuse for having a look—besides my curiosity.

I didn't see any signs of fire damage. Mrs. Sibley had mentioned that her handyman fixed all of that.

The scents got stronger as I moved toward the back of the store. My eyebrows went up when I flipped on more lights. There wasn't just a back storeroom, there was a complete workroom for soapmaking—or any kind of crafting. There was a rectangular worktable and dozens of shelves where ingredients and supplies might've been kept, a couple of large crocks and stainless-steel stock-sized pots still sitting on the workbench. A gas burner stove was built in for heating oils and lye. There was a large cutter for the finished bars.

I heard the bells on the door jingle a male voice call, "Hello…"

I exited the workroom and was surprised to see Nick Landry standing by the front door of the shop with a big grin. "Oh, hi." A little thrill ran through me when he smiled like that. Like his heart was always in his eyes.

He looked around. "I saw the door propped open. Whatcha doing in here?"

"Just having a look around. I spoke with Mrs. Sibley and picked up the keys. I was curious to see what smelled so good under my place."

"It does smell nice in here. Momma used to come and buy soaps and things."

"It must've been a popular place in town."

"Most definitely was. There were always shoppers in here when I drove by."

"I did a little cold-pressed soapmaking while my mom was sick after I'd had to quit my job to care for her. While she'd slept, I took some online classes. It became a hobby for a while."

"Sounds like you enjoyed doing it. Why did you stop?" Nick asked.

I lifted a shoulder. "Life happened and doing anything besides putting one foot in front of the other seemed impossible. My mom died, and then, shortly after that, I got sick."

"I'm sorry you had to go through all of that, but I'm not

sorry you're here now." He sounded sincere, and his kindness pulled at my heart.

"Thanks. I feel like I've got the opportunity for a fresh start here. Like anything is possible. The workroom back there had me itching to try my hand at a few batches of organic soaps."

"Maybe you could reopen the place with your own soaps."

I had to admit I got a tiny thrill at his suggestion. "I'm not a real soap maker, only a kitchen chemist. And I'm not ready to put down those kinds of roots here yet. It's a wait and see thing for me. I'm glad to be here for the holidays and to get to know the Bertrands better, but I'm kind of a square peg trying to fit in a round hole so far."

He appeared surprised at that. "I keep thinking you're here to stay."

"I'm here for now. Probably for at least a year before I decide where the future might take me." I didn't mention the codicil in the trust fund contract from Nana.

"Well, I hope you decide to stay, Allison. I have the feeling you could do anything you got set on doing."

"I appreciate the pep talk, Nick."

He lifted his nose in the air, same as I had just before he'd come in. "Wow, that does smell nice. Where is it coming from?"

"I'm not sure, but Mrs. Sibley said there were boxes of soap here." I stepped into the workroom and noticed a closed door. It was a closet with boxes stacked high. "I think we've found it."

I pulled out one opened box that had bars of soap. It was

labeled: *Honey and Pear*. It was divine. I passed the bar to Nick, who sniffed the wrapped bar. "That's nice."

"Did you know the owners?" I asked Nick.

He shook his head. "Can't say I did. In fact, I don't think they were from around here. I mean most everybody's from around here who lives here besides the students at the university and some of the professors. But I didn't know anything about the soap people."

He changed the subject. "Oh, and I stopped by to tell you that your car will be ready tomorrow. I was in the neighborhood and thought you'd want to know."

"Thanks for stopping by. So far, I haven't missed driving and haven't had to go anywhere beyond walking distance."

"I've got to head back to work, but I'll give you a call when I'm on the way with it."

"Great. See you tomorrow."

AFTER NICK HAD gone, I read some of the other labels on the boxes. *Lemon and Roses, Vanilla and Lavender, White Flowers.* I didn't open the boxes because they weren't mine, but I wanted to badly. As I turned off the lights and relocked the door, I realized that it had been too long since I'd used my creative skills to make something—or even decorate something—for that matter. The need to create was strong upon leaving the shop.

I brought the keys back to Mrs. Sibley, setting them quietly in the mailbox so as not to disturb her, but she suddenly appeared from behind her screened door. "Oh, hi there. Did you find what you were looking for?"

"It's a great retail space. Thanks again for letting me look around."

"Anytime, dear. Oh, and if you wanted to open a store, you know I'd give you a good rental rate."

"I appreciate your saying that, but I'm not quite sure where my life is headed these days." I hated to admit that, but it was true in every way.

"Of course. Let me know if I can help you with anything."

The afternoon was warm enough that I'd shed my jacket. I sat along the edge of the water on one of the many iron benches outside my apartment, watching the groups of friends and neighbors working together to get the lights put up.

The closest group seemed to be struggling untangling countless strings of lights, so I hopped up and offered to lend a hand.

A woman about my age noticed me and smiled. "I'm Kimmie. Thanks for helping."

I smiled back. "I'm Allison."

"We're down a couple volunteers today." She grimaced as if I would understand. I did, and I spent another hour testing and untangling lights at the nearby outlet. I hadn't thought about how many outlets one might need to light up an entire section of town like that.

"We're headed to grab a drink and some broiled oysters across the street. Would you like to join us, Allison?" a woman named Savannah asked.

It was only four o'clock, but I'd learned that "five o'clock somewhere" appeared to apply more to Louisiana than the Midwest. They were day drinkers, it seemed, and while I didn't have anything against a glass of wine or a craft beer, it was something else that had surprised me. "That sounds great. I've never tried an oyster."

"Oh, wow. Obviously you're from out of town given your accent," a guy named Jack said. "Where are you from?"

"I just moved here from Naperville, Illinois, near Chicago." I said this to the group as we all moved together toward the brick street in front of my loft. "I live up there." I pointed in the general direction of my place.

"No way. I'd give my sister away to live there." This comment came from Jack, but clearly he jested because a young woman named Izzy punched him in the arm. Both appeared to be of Creole descent. They had a similar skin color to Nick, with the same sprinkle of freckles.

"Well, thanks a lot."

"Just kidding, sis."

There were five of us who'd worked together to get the giant frame of an elf strung with lights. "So, Allison, can we put you on our decorating committee?"

Since I was currently out of work, what could it hurt? "Sure. I'd like that."

We crossed the street not far from the loft and took a right, heading down the block a short way until we heard loud music and laughter from a dive called Mama's Oyster Bar. The place was tiny, and several high-top tables were set up outside on the sidewalk, leaving just enough room for people to pass.

Since it was early, there were a couple empty four-top

tables, so we grabbed them and pushed them together to accommodate our group. "So, Allison, what do you do?" Savannah asked once we were seated.

"I was an interior designer back home. I also do space-planning for businesses."

"Lots of old houses to decorate around here."

The server took our order for drinks and appetizers.

"Yes, I love old homes. This town is gorgeous." I grinned, feeling included in this group of strangers who'd welcomed me. The breeze blew in from over the water, reminding me where I was and how my life had changed so quickly.

"My mom owns a design firm down the way," Kimmie said, pointing in the general direction. "She's looking for holiday employees through Christmas if you're looking for a job. You know, lots of wreath-making and arrangements. I can give you her contact information."

"Oh, wow. That would be fantastic. Thanks." I could do Christmas arrangements and wreaths with my eyes closed. I'd cut my teeth on them during an internship with a florist right after college.

The platters of broiled oysters arrived at the same time as our drinks. "These smell amazing." My mouth watered at the cloud of garlic, butter and Parmesan cheese that wafted up from the platter in front of me. "So, how does one eat an oyster?"

"Here, I'll show you." Jack lifted one of the almost-black shells that held the oyster and dipped it toward his mouth, where it slid right out of the shell in one bite. He then closed his eyes and moaned in obvious delight.

"That looks easy enough." I liked trying new foods, so I picked one up and imitated Jack's motion. The butter dripped onto my chin as I tried to determine if the salty, garlicky and a little bit gritty and slimy shellfish was something I wanted more of.

The others stared at me awaiting my verdict.

"I think I need another one to make a decision." They all laughed and cheered, and just as I slipped the second one in my mouth, I heard a familiar voice.

"Hey, everybody." Nick stood beside me and greeted the group. They all seemed to know and like one another, based on the backslapping and laughter.

His eyes focused on me then, as if he'd just noticed me sitting there. "Allison? It's nice to see you again so soon."

I grinned and wiped the butter from my chin. "You too, Nick."

"Allison just slurped down her first oysters." Jack sounded like a proud papa.

"Well, what did you think?" he asked me.

"Slimy, but pretty good. The garlic and cheese probably helped quite a bit."

"So, how do you two know each other?" Izzy asked. She had a hand on Nick's arm.

I told them the story of my car and how Nick had rescued me. "He was so kind to load all my stuff in his truck and bring me home."

"That's our Nick. Always a hero." Izzy smiled as she said the words, but somehow that smile didn't quite reach her gorgeous green eyes. *Did Nick and Izzy have a thing between them?*

Nick pulled up a stool beside me. "Did Allison tell you that she's Carly and Leah's big sister?" he questioned the group. Maybe he was trying to distract them from his choice of seating location.

All eyes landed on me with varying degrees of surprise, and maybe shock. I, in turn, slid him a look that said, *Thanks for throwing me under the bus.*

He shrugged and grinned. "The sooner it gets out, the sooner everybody moves on."

"I thought you looked familiar. You're a dead ringer for Leah," Kimmie said.

"Hmm, I think she looks more like Carly," Jack said.

"I can definitely see the resemblance to both of them," Izzy declared, her emotions back in check.

"So, what about Elizabeth? She's your sister too, right?" Jack asked.

"Um, yes, but we haven't gotten to know each other yet." Funny how everybody's eyes changed when Elizabeth was mentioned. Nobody said anything out loud about her, but body language and expressions were deafening. Nobody here liked my other sister—Elizabeth—much, from what I could tell.

"We're on team Leah, just so you know." Kimmie said this as if I should know what it meant.

"Team Leah?" I raised my brows in question.

"It's kind of a running joke for those of us who went to school with both of them. Elizabeth had a crush on Jake for years. And when Leah was living in France, Elizabeth made her move. She told everybody who would listen that they were an item. Some people in town believed it since they were friends, and because Jake's so nice that he didn't correct her."

So, one of my Bertrand sisters was in direct odds with the one on my father's side. "I guess I'm learning new things every day. I realize my family is…different, so please don't hold it against me, okay? I'm Switzerland." I held up my hands in submission. I could see the questions in their eyes. My family was interesting in strange ways that people wanted to find out more about.

"Welp, this is awkward," Izzy said. "Let's get another beer."

They all responded with a cheer at the suggestion, my family instantly forgotten…for the moment. But at least now I understood this new layer of enmity between my family members.

"I didn't expect to run into you," I said to Nick, though clearly, he had more reason to be here than I did.

"Well, these vultures are my friends and I help out when I can with the light stringing," Nick teased.

"Oh, Nick. We're not so bad," Jack cajoled him with a small shove to the shoulder.

"Nick's always super busy at the garage—he hardly comes out to play anymore." Izzy poked her lip out in an exaggerated pout.

"We all went to high school together, give or take a few grades up or down, so we meet up pretty often." Nick seemed at ease with his high school buddies, and not even a little put out with their ribbing.

"I guess I'll leave you to it. I've got some research to do." Then I turned to Kimmie. "Could I get your mom's contact information?"

"Sure. Hand me your phone and I'll enter it."

I unlocked the screen and passed it to where she was sitting.

Kimmie passed the phone back.

"Thanks for this, Kimmie."

"Sure. I'll tell Mom you're going to call."

"Allison, we're meeting just down from where we were today if you want to join in tomorrow. It won't be until a little later in the afternoon since we all have to work. Today, we managed to knock off early from our real jobs and get a head start. Except Nick." Kimmie teased Nick about his lack of availability.

"I'd love to." Being included warmed my soul. Having friends was something I hadn't realized I'd missed.

"Well, I'll be there tomorrow, so maybe we can do all of *this* again." He made a circular motion with his arms, indicating their group.

"Sounds good. See you then." I pulled my purse strap off the ladder-back stool and slung it over my shoulder.

CHAPTER SEVEN

"Hey. I'll walk you home." Nick caught up with me a few yards away.

"Oh. Okay. Thanks." He fell into step beside me. "What's with Izzy? She seems a little irritated we're hanging out." I didn't have the patience for jealous girlfriends.

He lifted a shoulder. "She and I went out in high school and a little in college. And occasionally after that, but we're in no way a couple. We decided we did better as friends."

"Maybe you decided. I don't want to cause any trouble." The last thing I needed was to make an enemy within this small group of new friends. Such tight-knit groups rarely made room for someone new, as thick as they were, so I felt lucky they'd invited me to join them.

"It's fine. We aren't together and haven't been for years."

It was getting colder now that the sun was setting early. The time had recently changed, making it darker an hour sooner in the evening. I shivered.

"You cold?" Nick was quick to ask. "Do you want my jacket?"

"No. I'm fine. It's only another block to my apartment."

We hurriedly covered the short distance to my place. As we arrived, Nick said, "I suggest maybe giving Elizabeth a shot. She isn't warm and fuzzy, but I've always had the impression she was lonely, despite her confidence. I can't think of one friend she has."

This had also been at the back of my thoughts. "I'll send her a message tomorrow. Maybe we can have lunch one day soon." It made me a little sad that Elizabeth wasn't well liked by people here in Cypress Bayou. Yes, she was prickly, but we all had our personality quirks, didn't we?

"Sorry to give so much unsolicited advice. Let me know if you want me to stop."

"It's nice having someone to talk to. Coming here, I realize how alone I am. I mean, I've got all this family, but it was nice meeting some new potential friends in town. Honestly, I'm a bit of a loner, mostly because I lived so many years with my mom. She and I were the best of friends." Before I thought better of it, I asked, "Would you like to come up for a glass of wine or a beer?"

"Sure. That would be nice." His grin was pretty rewarding.

Nick appeared to have taken a personal stake in helping me settle in here and it warmed me that he wanted to spend time with me. Despite his kindness and pretty great advice-giving, my family's stamp of approval took away some of the anxiety over becoming friends with someone new. Especially a guy.

I'd left the kitchen lights and a lamp on beside the sofa. "Come on in. I've got a cabernet and some assorted craft beers still in the fridge from Leah and Jake."

"I'll take a beer. Something pale if you've got it." He removed his jacket while I grabbed his beer and handed it to him across the island. He pulled up a stool while I grabbed a corkscrew from the drawer.

Also, thanks to Leah and Jake, I had several bottles of white wine in the fridge, and a couple reds on a rack in the kitchen. I hadn't yet gone grocery shopping, though I'd found the nearest store. There was still enough food in the refrigerator to get me through another day or two.

"The place looks a lot different since Leah moved in here. It was pretty basic back when it was only Jake and his roommate living here."

"Leah told me she'd gotten rid of a lot of his old college/bachelor guy stuff with Jake's blessing. She did a nice job with the place."

"So, what do you do in the evenings? TV? Online solitaire?" Nick was teasing me a little.

"I like TV and old movies. No solitaire, but maybe I should try it."

"Are you into reality TV?" he asked, making conversation.

"Mmm. Not so much, but I have been known to watch an awful lot of home and garden television. You?"

"No reality TV for me except sports. What's your favorite movie?"

I thought for a second. "I'd have to say *Grease*. Remember I said I liked old movies. My mom and I watched all the modern classics."

"I like musicals too. When you said old movies, I thought you meant *really* old movies."

"I like some of those too."

We chatted for a little while longer about favorite movies and shows while we finished our drinks. "Well, I've got an early morning tomorrow. Thanks for the beer."

I was becoming more and more attracted to Nick as I spent time with him. It wasn't only his smile or that he smelled good. I enjoyed his relaxed style, and he'd been deeply kind to me since I'd arrived in Cypress Bayou. He was refreshingly honest about who he was. And he was hot too. "Maybe we can do a movie night soon."

He paused a second from zipping his jacket and looked up at me, his expression hopeful. "I'd like that, Allison."

"I'll see you and Big Red tomorrow."

"Big Red?" He appeared puzzled initially, then a look of understanding entered his eyes. "Gotcha. You'd be surprised how many people name their vehicles."

"I probably would."

NICK WALKED BACK to his truck with a little spring in his step. He passed the oyster bar, but his friends were gone. He'd been surprised to see them all sitting with Allison today. Not that they weren't nice people, they just didn't usually invite outsiders into the group. They were all they needed most of the time.

It made him happy to think that Allison was getting to know a few people beyond the Bertrand family. She seemed to like Nana, Bob, and Leah quite a lot, but he could see how a few of the other personalities might be slightly more difficult. Carly was about ten years younger than Allison, so that might be a barrier. And Karen, well, she'd never been an easy person as far back as he could remember.

Nick had powered down his cell phone earlier to avoid distractions, and when he turned it back on, several messages popped up from his mom and two from garage employees.

Mom wanted him to stop by and have a slice of her homemade blueberry pie with ice cream. It was likely she'd heard he'd been hanging out with Allison, whom she'd not met yet. So, the invitation could be her wanting to get the latest about her neighbors, the Bertrands.

The messages from employees were the usual. One was sick, having to miss work tomorrow, and the other wanted to give Nick details about a vehicle brought in at the end of the day. Nick worked alongside his employees as a mechanic some days. Other days required him to run the business he would one day inherit. The Landry family owned and operated ten auto repair shops within a five-parish radius.

He'd learned the business of cars and fixing them since he was a kid. He didn't remember a time that he wasn't at the garage with his dad before and after school growing up. He'd gotten a business degree at Northwestern State University, or NSU, as it was referred to locally, and minored in accounting, and then an MBA. His dad had insisted on his getting the graduate degree, no matter that he preferred to be under the hood or the under the vehicle itself diagnosing and repairing. Nick had also completed several auto repair courses to learn the most up-to-date technology for fixing today's vehicles. Computers in cars were amazing, but an old-school mechanic would be out of luck trying to figure them out.

His friends kidded him about working so much, but there was no place he'd rather be than at the garage here in town. He'd had girlfriends besides Izzy over the years, but so far, they hadn't turned into anything long term, and he'd been disappointed by a few. Turns out, if a woman thought he was a simple mechanic instead of a business owner, she lost interest.

Nick hadn't mentioned to Allison the garages they owned, nor how hard he worked every day to make them a success. He still lived in the apartment over his parents' four-car garage because it was nice, and he didn't have any reason to move. From the outside, he appeared to be a simple, hardworking car mechanic. Nick understood that would probably suit him best, but he carried the lucky burden of the real world as well.

Allison appeared to enjoy his company, but she'd drawn an invisible line so far. She was new here and just getting her footing, and unfortunately, she wasn't sure if she planned to stay in Cypress Bayou permanently.

But she *had* suggested they do a movie night, so that was promising.

I WAS A little sad to see Nick leave. He was fun and thoughtful, and now the place felt kind of lonely. But today had been a good day. I'd met a few new potential friends, which was nice, but I didn't want to get too attached to Nick or anyone else. In my mind, moving here was a trial. A test to see if I could stomach a place so tightly knit and living so outside my Midwestern roots. Oh, and there was my family, who was a mixed bag so far.

I needed to be sure before I invested too much time and emotion here.

I decided it wasn't too late yet to give Kimmie's mom a call about temporary holiday work. Finding a job would give me an anchor and a schedule. I did better with structure.

"Hello?" a woman answered and a little bit of nerves kicked in. Maybe it *was* too late to call.

"Hi, this is Allison Miers. Kimmie shared your contact info with me and said that you might be looking for employees during the holiday season. I've just moved to town—"

Before I finished my sentence, the woman exclaimed, "Oh, yes! Kimmie called me earlier and said you might be contacting me. She shared that you were an interior designer in Chicago. I desperately need help with all the wreaths and arrangements. Can you stop by tomorrow morning around ten?"

"Yes. Thanks. I've got lots of experience in floral design. Where should I meet you?" I jotted down the address she rattled out.

"I'm looking forward to it, Allison."

So was I. I breathed a satisfied sigh at this small accomplishment. I hadn't realized how much stress I'd put on myself to find a job, even though it wasn't immediately necessary financially. I found such self-worth in my work. What I did, didn't change the world, but it meant a lot to me. And it had been far too long since I'd had the thrill of creating new things.

I was beginning to absorb the spirit of the holidays for the first time in a long time. Cypress Bayou at Christmas was shaping up to be a very good idea.

WHEN NICK TURNED into his parents' driveway, he noticed the Christmas lights strung neatly across the house and on the bushes and shrubs out front. Their giant oak's trunk had also been wrapped with clear white lights. He was surprised Mom hadn't asked him to help since he'd been hauling, moving, and fixing things around the house since he was a teen, alongside his dad. She must've hired someone to do it, since Dad still wasn't able to do any heavy lifting after his recent health issues. Mom liked having things done on her timetable, not liking to wait until someone got around to it.

The house was a red-brick historic Greek revival style with large white columns across the front. It resembled Nana's house but wasn't as large. The garage was adjacent to the house, built in the same style and separated by a short, covered walkway. It had been added to the original structure to house his father's special cars, with Nick's apartment on top.

He parked and entered the house and was greeted by Buddy, the old hound they'd had since he'd been a senior in high school. Buddy now split time between staying at his parents' house, at the garage most days, and his apartment. Some days, Buddy struggled with the stairs, reminding them that he wouldn't live forever.

"Hey, Buddy. Were you a good boy today? Yes, you were." Nick did his usual petting and crooning to his old pal. Buddy's tail wagged and he slobbered on Nick's hand.

"Hello, dear. Come on in. I've got a slice of pie with your name on it." His mom wore pearls with her navy pantsuit.

"Hey, Mom. Did y'all eat out?" Nick was only mildly curious. His parents went out a lot.

"Only to the Kellers' house for dinner. You know, they're not socializing much right now because of all that unpleasantness a few months back."

Nick made a face. "I'd say it was unpleasant. Unpleasant for that poor woman whose freedom they stole to save their own skin." His mom's ability to understate was legend.

"There were extenuating circumstances. And everybody knows Carson Carmichael was to blame." Mom waved the horror away with a flick of her hand.

Carson Carmichael was Tanner and Jake Carmichael's father, and a prominent lawyer here in Cypress Bayou. It was easy to blame him for pretty much every terrible thing that happened in town. He'd done a lot of awful things, but there were others who bore responsibility for some of it. Including Allison's biological father, Judge Keller.

"Mom, Carson Carmichael and Judge Keller declared a woman incompetent and had her committed to a mental institution to make her seem crazy just to keep their secret. The judge was an active participant and had just as much to lose as Carson."

"That's not the way I've heard it straight from Arthur's own mouth. He and Tootie are laying low because of all the negative publicity surrounding them—and because it's gotten out that he fathered Karen Bertrand's child."

"Yes, and speaking of that: her name is Allison, and she's a lovely person."

"A little bird told me you came to her rescue when she

got into town. I guess you've seen her recently?" His mother's stare was like truth serum—always had been.

"We just met a few days ago."

"Well, that's a relief because you know that Elizabeth would have a fit." Mom referenced the judge's daughter, and Allison's other half sister.

"Why on earth would Elizabeth care if Allison and I were friends, or dating for that matter?"

"She's not ready to declare that she even has a sister, and we're close to the family, you know. That includes you."

"We're not exactly good friends, Mom." Elizabeth was a few years younger than him, and they'd never been especially close, despite their parents' relationship. But he'd always believed Elizabeth was more spoiled and misunderstood rather than the pariah most considered her.

"Well, we're all friends, and I'm still a friend to Karen Bertrand, so it puts me in an awkward position sometimes."

"So, I'm assuming you're trying to help." Mom did enjoy drama, even though she might not intend to hurt anyone with her busybody behavior.

She drew back in an offended posture. "Of course, I would never abuse my relationships with anyone. It's just hard sometimes because I hear both sides."

"There shouldn't be any *sides*, Mom. That's my point. What happened so many years ago is fact. And now that it's out, the chatter about it has the power to affect lives, Allison's life, now that she's moved to town. She's the innocent victim here. I'm just asking you to be kind and remember these are real people."

"I'll do my best to use my powers for good. How's that?"

"Excellent. Now, you mentioned pie?"

"I kept it warm for you. I'm assuming you prefer it à la mode?"

"Is there any other way to eat blueberry pie?"

CHAPTER EIGHT

THE BELLS ON the door jingled as I entered *Donavan Interiors*, and a woman wearing glasses low on her nose looked up, a wreath hanging from one arm, her expression harried. "Are you Allison?" she asked.

"Hi, yes, I'm Allison." I noticed the festive accessories and furniture set up in vignettes within the retail space. In here, it was already Christmas. "Your store is lovely."

"Thanks. I'm Lydia Donovan. I'm glad you could come in today. Yesterday, just before closing, I received an order for fifty artificial wreaths with angels and bells and bows to be delivered to the city council in three days. Can you help me?" She led me into the back workroom, which was almost as large as the store.

"Right now? I have my résumé, if you'd like to see it," I offered, holding up the single sheet of paper tucked away in a slim black folder.

Lydia waved away my words and my vitae. "I can look at it later. Here's a photo to follow. They should all look pretty much the same, with everything wired on tightly, as they're going to be hung along the bridge over the bayou."

I took the photo from her hand and decided it wouldn't be a difficult task. "Okay. I can do it."

"The wreaths are all stacked here, along with the accessories to make them. I locked up and ran out to get the supplies as soon as I got the request yesterday. I've got dozens of other orders to work on, but I couldn't turn the council down. I'm thrilled that you've come to my rescue, Allison."

I put my purse down, took off my jacket, and rolled up my sleeves. I peered at the photo and memorized numbers and positioning of the items to affix. There were plastic bins filled with supplies. "Okay. I've got this." I hadn't made any other plans until late afternoon, so this worked out.

"I'm not a florist, but I do get asked to craft a lot of fresh and artificial holiday arrangements come the season," Lydia said, maybe to help clarify why she had so many floral orders.

"I'll get started then." I was already mentally calculating how long each wreath might take. I almost always set a goal when I had this kind of job to do. Maybe four per hour?

"Oh, and I'll pay you twenty dollars an hour. Does that work?"

I nodded. "That works." I'd made more at the store where I worked in Naperville, and when I'd made calls to clients' homes, it was a substantially higher rate. But I realized temporary holiday workers didn't earn as much, and I was eager to make connections here in the business.

Since I didn't have rent due for a while, I'd worry about something more permanent soon so I didn't have to dip into my savings. I pulled up a stool and positioned the bells, angels, and bows where I could sit in one spot at the worktable and put the wreaths together assembly-line style.

I made the first one and held it up for Lydia's approval.

"Wow. That was fast, and it looks great." I could see the tiny frown of stress drop from her expression. "So, what else are you good at, Allison?"

We talked while we worked. "I've worked in an interiors shop for years, so we did floral arrangements, visited clients in their homes to consult and bid on jobs, and did space design. Most residential, but some business."

"Sounds like you're way overqualified for this, but I'm thrilled to have you here. I normally have another couple of employees, but one is out on maternity leave and the other has the flu."

"I'm sorry to hear that. I met Kimmie when I pitched in to help with the Christmas lights yesterday. Apparently, they've got a couple of their volunteers down with the flu as well."

"So, Kimmie tells me you're the latest addition to the Bertrand family."

Her easy words caused me to pause for a second. It seemed so simple for people to talk about me when they didn't know me. Lydia's tone was conversational, as if she didn't feel strange asking about it. "Um, yes. I guess it was a shock to people in town to learn about me."

"Not so much a shock, as it's fascinating to learn something new. It makes us all see Karen Bertrand in a new light."

I wasn't exactly sure what she meant by that, and I didn't want to ask. I had no intention of adding any fodder to their gossip mill. I realized that I felt protective of Karen and the rest. "The family has been very kind to me."

"I expect nothing less. They are good people." Lydia

sounded sincere, so I decided to leave it at that, where my family was concerned, for the moment. I instead focused on producing as many wreaths as possible, as well as possible.

After a couple of hours, I stood to release tension in my back. "Feel free to grab some lunch when you get hungry," Lydia said from across the worktable where she was working on a large, artificial festive arrangement. I had to admit, the woman had skills.

"Do you have any suggestions for a quick lunch nearby?" I asked.

"The Cane River Café is about a half a block down to your right as you walk out. They have gumbo, po' boys, and other kinds of sandwiches and soups."

"Okay, I'll give them a try." I finished up the wreath I'd been working on and picked up my purse. "Can I get you anything?"

"I've brought my lunch today, so I'm good. Thanks. Take your time."

I strolled down the sidewalk, noticing the Christmas decorations going up in the windows of the shops I passed. I'd often been hired to do storefront design for Naperville's larger stores, so I was interested in watching the progress. It was beginning to look a lot like Christmas around here.

After I ordered a shrimp po' boy with a side of red beans and rice, I moved aside to wait and let others order. I noticed a couple of people staring at me curiously. Then I remembered how much I looked like Leah, so I figured that's what it must be. "Allison?"

I looked up from my phone to stare into the eyes of a tall, blond woman. "Can I help you?"

"It's me, Elizabeth Keller." The woman cocked a brow, as if I was addlebrained. She was the last person I expected to run into.

I blinked. "Oh, hi. How are you?" I'd seen her photo online but hadn't met her in person. In person, she was prettier than her photos. But we didn't really resemble one another, except maybe our noses?

"Well, isn't this awkward? I heard you'd arrived in town. I'm surprised you haven't called or texted me and Daddy." She had a hand on her hip, lightly tapping a very high-heeled nude pump, an impatient gesture.

"I've only been here a couple of days." I said this hoping it was a good enough explanation. Truth was, I hadn't considered contacting either of them right away. I would've eventually.

"I'll bet you've seen all the Bertrands, haven't you?" She continued the shoe-tapping.

Oh, this was going to be a thing. "Well, yes. They had a big part in persuading me to move here. They got me a place to live and helped me get settled." I felt the need to defend them all. It's not like Elizabeth had offered to help or contacted me.

"Well, I guess we're a big embarrassment to you. Daddy's got his feelings hurt." She said it in a challenging tone that put me on edge. Such a manipulative tactic.

"I wasn't trying to hurt anyone, Elizabeth. I've just arrived, and my car broke down, so I'm on foot. I was planning to contact you both soon." That was true-ish.

The person behind the counter called my name, so I stepped around Elizabeth. "Excuse me. That's my order."

"It's okay. I'll wait." But she immediately looked down at her very expensive watch.

I stepped away and took the bag from the server, who gave me a look of pity, or maybe solidarity, as Elizabeth hadn't bothered keeping a hushed tone. *Did everyone in this town know everything about me?*

The moment I stepped back, Elizabeth said, "I was going to call you today. We'll expect you for dinner at seven tomorrow night at the house. Mother has decided it's time to bring you into the fold. That's nice of her, isn't it?"

I had no idea how to respond to that. But I did recognize that I was being bullied in the middle of a café. Instead of reacting badly, I made a show of pulling up the calendar on my phone, so Elizabeth understood that I didn't take orders from her. "Yes. Okay. I can do tomorrow night. Send me the address." I knew she had my number. "See you then."

"I'll let Momma know to expect you." Elizabeth's gaze was triumphant, and her foot stopped tapping.

Without hesitating a moment more, I exited the establishment, walked a little way, crossed the street, and then dropped down on one of the benches that overlooked the bayou. I took several deep breaths and calmed my mind. When I was sick, I'd learned to let things go that I couldn't control, and I'd done nothing to cause Elizabeth's rude behavior. Or maybe, it was just her normal behavior based on what I'd picked up from others around town.

There had been enough remarks made to me about Elizabeth by near strangers since I'd come here that I was beginning to understand the reasons for their comments. I wouldn't let her bother me. I wouldn't. After all, she didn't even ask how I was or welcome me to Cypress Bayou.

But I'd agreed to step into her territory for dinner tomorrow night with her parents. How had that even happened? I was a pleaser at heart and hated conflict—always had—so of course I'd agreed. Shaking it off, I began eating my lunch, wondering what the Kellers were like.

Staring out across the water, I noticed the progress of the volunteers in setting up the Christmas light displays. It was amazing, I had to admit. The number of large lit pieces had doubled at least in the past two days. Which reminded me that I'd offered my help to my new friends and Nick string lights later today. Since I wouldn't be finished with the wreaths by then, I texted Nick to let him know.

He replied: *Congrats on the new job. We can meet after we're all done and grab a bite if you want.*

Sounds fun. I assume I'll get off work around six or so. Lydia hadn't specified a time, but I figured if she wanted me to work later, she would have said so.

I'll meet you there and we can walk someplace together.

A little thrill ran through me at the thought of seeing Nick again. And I loved that I could walk to almost everything I needed or wanted. It was different than where I'd lived before. Add that to the plus column.

I re-entered the workroom to find Lydia eating a sandwich at her workstation. She glanced up when I pulled my up stool to start on the wreaths again. "Oh, hey, how was lunch?"

"Great. I had a shrimp po' boy and sat by the water for a few minutes." I avoided mentioning the unexpected run-in with my sister.

"That place has the best po' boys. I have to be careful not to eat there too often. The food is fabulous but not especially low calorie."

"It was a wonderful treat."

"I understood you were recovering from cancer. How are you doing with that?"

"Thanks. I'm getting better all the time. Almost back to normal." It occurred to me then that it was on me to get used to being an open book. Rolling my eyes or refusing to answer their questions wouldn't help me fit in here.

"Please let me know if I try and work you too hard. This is the busy season and I tend to overdo it sometimes, especially since I'm understaffed now."

"Thanks. So far, I've felt pretty good since I've gotten to town." I tried not to sound resentful. And I wasn't—exactly.

I suddenly felt a kinship with my two brothers-in-law, having to go through daily life with everybody talking about their father behind their backs. And Leah's bone marrow donation to me, which started it all. Now, the residents had all kinds of interesting topics to discuss. On both sides of my new family.

NICK WORKED THROUGH lunch and took off just in time to meet his friends at the agreed-upon spot on the bank of the bayou. He shed his jacket almost immediately, as the sun had warmed things up since the early chill this morning. He'd grabbed a ladder on his way out the door from the garage.

Savannah and Jack were already there, but Izzy and

Kimmie hadn't arrived yet. "Hey y'all."

"Glad you could make it today, bro." Jack gave him a fist bump. "Thanks for bringing the ladder."

"Yeah, we don't see too much of you when the sun is shining lately," Savannah said. It was only four thirty, but it got dark around five these days, so they had a couple of spotlights to help them see what they were doing in the dark.

"You know how it is. The family business is pretty much mine now." His dad had officially turned things over to Nick just about a year ago when he'd unexpectedly had open-heart surgery. It had scared his mom so much that she'd insisted it was time for him to retire.

"How's your dad?" Savannah asked.

"He's taken to gardening this year like it's his job. Stays out of Mom's way as best he can." Nick didn't blame his father, since Nick pretty much did the same, staying out of her way. Mom was notorious for finding projects for other people to do. And living over their garage sometimes made Nick an easy target.

"So, what's with you and Allison, the new girl? She's hot." Jack was probably tasked by his sister, Izzy, to ask the question.

"We hit it off the day she got to town. She's nice, but since we just met, we're not really a thing."

"What time's she going to be here?" Savannah asked.

"Oh, she said to tell y'all that she's helping Mrs. Donovan at her shop today but can meet us after. I'm assuming she's been hired to do holiday work."

"Mrs. Donovan has the energy of three people in their twenties. And Kimmie says she's short-staffed this year.

Sounds like our new friend is going to be as busy as you are, Nick."

Kimmie and Izzy arrived, with Kimmie hauling a wagon filled with Christmas lights and Izzy holding several large surge suppressors. "Hey, everybody." Izzy's eyes met Nick's and he had a sudden urge to look away. He read expectation and hope in them whenever they were together these days. He'd moved on, but maybe she hadn't as much.

"Where's Allison?" Izzy asked.

Nick told her about Allison's new job with Kimmie's mom.

"Yeah, Mom just got a huge order from the city for a bunch of wreaths. I'm glad Allison was able to help."

"Yeah. Me too." Izzy said this without obvious snark, but he wasn't sure if Izzy was pleased that Allison could help Mrs. Donovan, or that she was simply happy Allison wasn't here today.

"Y'all should have seen my class today. They drew what they wanted their Christmas trees to look like. My faves were the pink, purple, and black ones. Some even had swords. I'm guessing their parents won't take most of their suggestions." Kimmie was the best kindergarten teacher around and filled with so much excitement for her job.

"I'll bet. What is it with the swords?" Savannah smiled.

"It's a fantasy for kids. They're all ninjas in their imaginations, except the ones who will always be princesses." Jack said this as if he understood. "I've got a sword or two in my past."

They all laughed at that. "We believe you, Dungeon Master." Izzy gave him a hard time about his continued fixation with Dungeons and Dragons. "You need to find yourself a Dungeon Mistress, or you'll be single forever."

"Working on that."

"Nick, what are you doing for Thanksgiving?" Izzy asked.

"No plans yet. Probably just eat until we all pass out like we always do." Thanksgiving was next week, and he'd not given it much thought.

CHAPTER NINE

"Oh, hi, Nick. What brings you here?" Lydia greeted him warmly. When Nick showed up at six o'clock, I was still knee-deep in Christmas wreaths.

I looked up when I heard his voice. I'd been so involved with finishing my personal goal that I'd completely lost track of time.

"I'm meeting up with Allison after work."

"Hey there. I've got one more to finish." Then, I swung my gaze over to Lydia. "If that's all right with you?"

"Of course, dear. You've gotten more done today than I did. I'd swear you've been doing this kind of work your whole life. The wreaths look fantastic."

"You did all of these today?" Nick looked at my stack of completed greenery and appeared impressed.

"Yes. Once I get going, I lose track of time."

"With Allison here, I might not need any other employees."

"Okay, this is the last one." I affixed a big red bow with wire onto the wreath I was working on.

"Excellent. What time can you come tomorrow?" Lydia asked.

"Eight?"

"Perfect. See you then. Y'all have fun. And if you see my

daughter, tell her to call her mother."

"Will do, Mrs. Donovan." Nick nodded as he helped me with my coat.

We started along the sidewalk toward my apartment. "I've made a dinner reservation if that's all right."

This surprised me a little. "Oh, okay. I thought we would be meeting up with the group."

"They all ended up having other things to do, so we decided to split up after we finished today."

"Should I change my clothes?" I wasn't sure how nice this restaurant might be.

"No, but we've got a little time before our reservation, so if you want to freshen up after your busy day, we can stop by your place first."

"So, the jeans are okay?"

He looked at my jeans. "Those jeans are perfect."

I staunched the urge to giggle at his words. It had been a long time since anyone had flirted with me.

"Okay. The jeans stay, but I'm going to change my top." We arrived at my apartment then and I climbed the stairs, aware of Nick right behind me.

"Can I get you a glass of wine?" he asked, once we were inside.

"Sure. There's an open red on the counter. Help yourself to anything you want in the kitchen. Beers are in the fridge." I pointed. "Oh, and where are we going to dinner?"

"Someplace where you can wear your jeans, so don't get too fancy."

He handed me a generous pour of cabernet. "Gotcha." I headed toward my bedroom thinking about what I might wear.

NICK WATCHED HER go. He'd made the last-minute reservation for dinner at the Marina on Breaux Lake. It sat on pylons at the end of a pier over the water and provided a gorgeous sunset for diners, no matter the season. He figured Allison hadn't gone that far to the outskirts of town yet, either of the other times, so it would be a nice change of scenery for her.

She re-entered the room within minutes, having chosen a royal-blue satin top paired with her same jeans. "Nice shoes." Her wineglass was empty.

"Thanks. I rarely wear anything besides boots or comfortable shoes these days since I haven't been anywhere lately. I'm assuming we're not walking." She held up her foot, showing him her dressier footwear for the evening.

"You look fantastic. And we're driving. You ready?"

She grabbed her jacket from beside a hook by the door. "I am."

He helped her into the passenger's side of his truck and let his fingers linger on hers a second longer than was necessary. She looked up at him in question.

"I hope you didn't think I tricked you into a date."

She smiled, her cat hazel eyes shining. "I'll allow it this once."

They drove through town past the university, and Allison watched the rows of old and new buildings and dormitories as they passed. "Wow, this place is bigger than I thought.

How many students attend?" she asked.

"Roughly eleven thousand undergrad students, which is more than when I attended. Not sure about the graduate student numbers."

Allison's eyebrows rose at that.

"Are you surprised that I'm a college graduate?" he asked.

"Maybe a little, because I only know you as my new friend and excellent car mechanic."

"My parents insisted on my getting an education." Insisted was a mild word. His mother wouldn't hear of anything less than a postgraduate degree, which only his closest friends knew about.

"My mom did too. I have an undergraduate degree in design with a double major in business."

As Nick pulled into the parking lot, Allison caught sight of the lake surrounding the restaurant. "This is so cool, Nick. Which lake is this?"

"It's called Breaux Lake. It's small, but big enough to water-ski and boat on."

"I've never water-skied before. It looks like such fun."

"We all grew up on the water. Skiing, fishing, boating. It's how we entertain ourselves in the hot summer months here."

"I heard Carly say something similar. I've heard that she and Tanner sometimes go fishing when they're working on a tough case together."

"It helps to live on the bayou with a boat at the ready." Nick loved to fish and someday he hoped to have such a convenient setup.

"It amuses me that they live in an Airstream trailer together. That's some serious togetherness."

Nick laughed. "I said the same thing when they got together, seeing how they also work together all day."

"They seem happy."

Nick led Allison up the small wooden deck to the front door of the restaurant.

They were met by the host, his former classmate, Jeff, who'd recently come out with his partner, Paul. "Oh, hey there, Nicky. I saw you'd made a reservation for tonight. It's been a minute since I've seen you, my friend."

"Great to see you, man. This is my new friend, Allison Miers."

"Oh girl. You've got a familiar look to you. Have you been in before?" Jeff narrowed his eyes at Allison.

Since it would take only another five seconds before Jeff figured it out, possibly loudly, Nick said, "Allison is Carly and Leah's sister, and she's just moved into town from Illinois."

Recognition flooded Jeff's eyes. "Oh, yes! Now I see it. Honey, we've heard about you around here, but I guess you know that by now. Welcome to Cypress Bayou." He touched Allison on the arm.

Allison, bless her, smiled, and said, "Thanks." Nick understood how uncomfortable she was with all the attention since coming here.

"I was saving the corner table in case the mayor showed up but looks like it's your table tonight. Best seats in the house. Welcome, Allison."

"Thanks, Jeff." Nick slapped Jeff on the back in a gesture of friendship.

"It's the least I can do since you always give me a discount on my oil changes. Oh, and for our new friend here. Love those Bertrand girls."

Jeff led them to the table that overlooked the back corner with water on both sides. The pinks, oranges, and yellows of the setting sun starkly contrasted the dark blue clouds gathering. "Looks like we might get some rain."

"It's a lovely view, Nick. Thanks for bringing me here."

WE ORDERED THE daily special of crawfish étouffée over rice, green salad, and garlic bread. "This is one of my favorites. Nana cooks it often, and hers is divine."

"I've not had a bad experience here yet, so hopefully it will be almost as good as Nana's recipe." We shared a bottle of chardonnay and a dozen oysters while waiting for our entrees.

"So, I thought we could stop by and pick up your car on the way home from the shop."

"Yes. I nearly forgot that it was supposed to be ready today. I've enjoyed walking everywhere in town, so I didn't miss it nearly as much as I might have in Naperville."

"I'm assuming that's a good thing to not notice. But with the rain in tomorrow's forecast, you'll be glad to have your car back."

"I hadn't even thought about it raining. I've gotten used to not planning for the immediate future. But checking the weather forecast might come in handy."

"So, why *did* you decide to move here? I mean, it doesn't

seem like it's something you'd do considering what I've learned about you."

I took a sip of my wine, deciding how much I should tell Nick about my personal life that he didn't already know. "There was a stipulation in Nana's trust fund agreement that I had to stay for one year."

His eyes widened. "Diabolical."

I laughed at his response. "Yes. Pure extortion." I doubted my trust fund was a secret around town. People liked to talk about such things.

"So, how do you feel about that? As shrewd as I know Nana is, I'm surprised that was her play."

I waved that off. "It's payback as far as I'm concerned. They took me in when I didn't have anyone and was in dire need of help. So, if she wants to extort me a little to make me give them a chance, then, I guess I'm okay with it. It's not like I've got anything else happening in my life right now."

Our server brought out the entrees and we paused our conversation temporarily. "This smells so good."

"Hmm."

"Conflict hater, huh? Now I get why your two new families are so daunting to you."

"I love that you use that word."

"Have I said it before?" He appeared surprised.

"Yes, the first day we met. And you were also referencing my family when you said it."

Nick held up his glass. "Here's to things becoming less daunting in your life."

I lifted my glass, tapping his. "I'll accept that toast."

"So, are you working at the shop tomorrow?"

Allison nodded. "As far as I know I'll be working every weekday and some Saturdays leading up to Christmas. But tomorrow evening I'm supposed to go to the Kellers' house for dinner. Elizabeth cornered me at the café this afternoon and insisted."

"Oh, wow. I hope that goes well."

"I'm going to bring a bottle of wine and my patience."

"Good call. Might want to bring two bottles. Tootie Keller can sling back the vino."

"I'll keep it in mind."

CHAPTER TEN

NICK WONDERED HOW the dinner would go tomorrow night for Allison. The Kellers weren't an easy bunch, but it was up to her and them to forge a way forward. As much as he'd like to fill her in completely about the family, the scandal surrounding the judge, and Elizabeth's behavior over the years, Nick held off. He'd stuck his nose into her private affairs maybe a little too much already.

Nick felt protective of her, and they barely knew each other. She was stunning, to say the least, but it was more than that. Her air of vulnerability and inexperience fascinated him. She was thirty-five and had spent the last several years caring for her mother and then fighting cancer. Not that he was judging. He still lived above his parents' garage.

"Your car is working fine now, so let me know if you have any more trouble with it." They'd left the restaurant and were headed toward his shop.

"I will. Thanks again for helping me. And for being my first friend in town."

"Of course. I'm sorry to be too nosy."

"I don't exactly have secrets. More like a series of unpleasant circumstances these past couple of years. And I probably didn't handle things as well as I could have."

"I'm sure you did what you thought best at the time.

And I'll work on minding my own business in the future."

"I'm not upset with you. In fact, I haven't had anyone to talk to about any of this, so maybe you've come at a good time. I feel somewhat lighter having told somebody about it."

"So, how would you feel about that movie night?" he asked, and realized he was holding his breath waiting for her response.

"Sounds like fun to me. I'm in."

"Okay, I guess it's only fair that you come over to my place. I don't know what your setup is, but I've got *all* the channels. Send me a list of your favorite movies and I'll make sure I can get them all."

"Okay, I'll bring some snacks and drinks."

"It's a date." He hadn't exactly meant to say that. But honestly, he hoped she didn't take issue with it.

Allison's cheeks flushed a pretty pink. "Okay, then."

He pulled into the shop's parking area. "Hang on, I've got your keys inside."

"Thanks."

He jogged to the side entrance of the building and disengaged the alarm system. The smell of oil, gasoline, and rubber from the tires hit him as he entered—as it always did. He loved that smell.

He kind of regretted telling Allison about his college degree. He'd wanted to impress her in that moment. But she was likely more confused by it than anything. Why would she think a car mechanic would have that kind of education and still work on cars? Would she think he was an underachiever?

If he met someone new who showed an interest in him, Nick usually paid close attention to how she responded when he told her he was a car mechanic. And how much more interested she became on finding out he ran the family business and had an MBA.

But so far, Allison was different. She hadn't seemed to mind his *only* being a mechanic.

He grabbed her keys from the hook and locked back up.

Allison climbed out of his truck and met him in the parking lot next to where he'd parked her car. "Did you wash it? It looks great."

"I had my guy detail it. Just a little perk for knowing your mechanic."

She smiled at him. "Thank you so much. I haven't had it deep-cleaned in ages. I'm a little embarrassed by the condition of it, honestly."

"Ah, it was nothing a good spit shine didn't cure."

"Well, I'm thrilled to have her back."

"Are you okay to drive home from here?" he asked, even though she'd only had one and a half glasses of wine.

"Of course." She looked at him a little funny. "You know I'm thirty-five, right?" He felt himself doing it again, being protective of her.

"Sorry. For some reason I feel like I should see you home safely."

"Well, you don't need to, but thanks for all you've done for me. Please let me know how much I owe you for the parts and labor."

He waved a hand toward the shop. "Our receptionist will contact you about an invoice."

"Great. I had a nice time tonight. I'll see you in a couple of days. Just send me your address."

"I'm looking forward to finding out what kind of dark and twisty kinds of stuff you like to watch."

"Not too twisty, but I do like a little weird and creepy here and there."

"My kind of girl."

IT FELT STRANGE, but nice, to be back behind the wheel again. My car smelled fresh and clean, and it made me smile that Nick had gone to the extra effort on my behalf.

I parked across from my apartment, on the bayou side of the street, and stared out over the water along the bank where I noticed several new colorfully lit pieces. The lights were spectacular, and I couldn't wait to see them all turned on at the same time. Until my dad died, he'd always put up lights on the outside of our house, and now, seeing these made me think of him and miss my parents even more. I thought about seeing my birth father tomorrow night, whom I'd only been introduced to once, briefly. I couldn't imagine his bringing me into his family the way the Bertrands had done.

I climbed the stairs to my apartment feeling a little empty and lost, needing to belong someplace. I'd always thought that by now I might have my life more figured out, at least more than I currently did.

My new home was silent, with the soft sounds of cars passing by every few seconds. I flipped on the light and noticed my yellow list of reasons to and not to move sitting on the edge of the bar amongs a stack of other papers I'd recently pulled out to go through.

I'd made the list out of sheer uncertainty and moved based on the results of my balance sheet. I picked up the page, now a little frayed at the corners, and stared at it.

Plusses:
My new family
I'd not be alone
The weather
The food
Something new in my life (change)
Jake Carmichael would be nearby in case I got sick again

Minuses:
My new family
I would miss my home
No snow at Christmas (this was a questionable drawback)

And so it went on. And while the positives didn't far outweigh the negatives, at least my decision was based on something concrete. Some good reasons to make this move that I'd thought hard about before relocating.

I decided that I was okay having a date or two with Nick. We were casual and taking it slow, and I'd decided he was a good guy.

I'D SLEPT POORLY and made it to the store with only a minute or two to spare. For some reason, the move just now seemed to be catching up with me. Chemo had walloped me, and some days I had a hard time sleeping, concentrating, or staying out of bed. I'd waited to sell Mom's house until I thought I could handle the changes both mental and physical.

"Hey there, Allison. You okay?" Lydia Donovan eyeballed me, and obviously noticed my meaty eyes.

"Yes. I'm okay." I tried not to be a complainer. Nobody wanted to hear about somebody else's aches and pains. "I didn't sleep well last night is all."

"If you're not feeling well, you have to let me know."

"I will, Lydia. Thanks. Just a lack of sleep. I'll make it up tonight." I put my purse and jacket down on the stool next to me. "So, what are we working on today?"

"Well, the city council was so thrilled with our quick turnaround of the wreaths, they ordered some greenery for the utility poles downtown. You know, the old-looking streetlamps? But they don't want wreaths."

"That's great. Did they specify exactly what they want?" I asked.

"They asked that we come up with some ideas, so if you've got something fun in your creative brain, let me know."

"I'm assuming they want artificial since it's still so early." I ticked through some of the things I'd done in the past. "Hmm. Maybe boughs or swags."

"Either would work."

"I'll think about it while I work on these." The distraction allowed me to *not* think about my new and uncertain life." I looked down at the stack of paper with hand-written notes in front of me. Lydia appeared to trust me with her clients' orders, because I had a pile of them in front of me at my workstation.

"Oh, and Mrs. Jeffries doesn't want anything too sparkly or lit for that table arrangement. And she hates poinsettias."

"Got it." Thankfully, Lydia was well-stocked with other stems and greenery. I began working on the others while allowing my mind to formulate new ideas. I did my best thinking while I worked. "So, what if we did something like this?" I held up a small swag threaded with some small holly berries, a single silver bow, and a few jingle bells hanging down.

"Hmm. Yes, that might work. Here, let me snap a quick photo and send it to them. The sooner we decide, the sooner I can get the supplies."

"I managed the store where I worked before, so if you need me to deal with vendors and orders, I can do that." Doing florals was fun, but I did want Lydia to know that I could readily run her shop, should she need me to.

"You're so good at all of it. I can see the experience in everything you do here."

"Thanks." I blushed a little at her praise.

The two of us worked steadily all morning. "Would you like to go out and get lunch today?" Lydia asked me.

"Oh. Sure. Is it lunchtime already?" I'd hardly looked up from my work, but now noticed how many orders I'd done. They were lined up along the table. Losing myself in creative work allowed my mind to relax.

"There's a farmer's market today through the weekend. I thought we might stop in and see what they've got."

I loved farmer's markets. "I used to go to one back home every Friday."

"Well, we need to get out of here and get some fresh air anyway. They'll have booths with food."

"Sounds great." I grabbed my coat and purse and followed Lydia to the front door. Lydia seemed to be warming up to me. She'd rarely mentioned or questioned me about my family since the first day, so I guess we were making progress with mutual respect.

I was looking forward to my movie night with Nick tomorrow evening but feeling a little anxious as well. Maybe there would be something special at the farmer's market I could bring to his house. Tonight's dinner with the Kellers was a different story. I was dreading it, quite frankly. Elizabeth put me on edge.

CHAPTER ELEVEN

I LEFT WORK just after five o'clock. The wind was blustery, and the temps were dropping, as forecasted, so I'd driven to work. Walking in cold rain wasn't my favorite thing to do. This wasn't Chicago, after all, and I was quickly adapting to *not* being there it seemed.

I questioned whether I should go ahead and have a glass of wine before getting ready for my evening with the Kellers. A small part of my brain had been worrying all day about tonight's dinner. I wasn't sure which concerned me most: the idea of being in the same room with my prickly sister or my outlaw-judge father. Or, maybe his wife, from whom he'd kept my existence a secret for thirty-five years.

I dressed carefully, having gotten the impression that these weren't casual people. Elizabeth was one of the few women who proudly strutted around town in expensive designer shoes and clothes. I'd noticed that most of the women here didn't dress up on a regular day. I saw lots of jeans, boots, and sweaters, and yes, even a little camo. Of course, most weren't cardiothoracic surgeons who looked like six-foot-tall models.

I chose my favorite winter-white jeans and paired them with a soft, cashmere cowl-neck sweater in a brick color. My rust-colored suede ankle boots were slim, with a medium heel. I wore my mom's favorite heart-shaped pendant with tiny diamonds all around.

It was a simple outfit, but elegant enough to pass muster. Unless they *dressed* for dinner, which nobody I knew ever did. Then, I could pass if off as their being extravagant. I would be kind, polite, and eat whatever they put in front of me, just like my mom taught me.

I'd known it was coming, this facing of my past and future. I only hoped I was strong enough to go toe-to-toe with this branch of my new family. I'd kicked cancer's butt so far, and I couldn't imagine dinner with the Kellers could be harder than that. I grabbed two bottles of wine: a red and a white, for good measure.

I'd just gotten in my car when a text from Nick came through. *Good luck tonight! You've got this!* ☺

Nick's simple words bolstered me a little, causing me to sit up a little straighter and tap into my reserves of strength. *Thanks for the boost of confidence* ☺

See you tomorrow night at my place. Send me your movie choices. Oh, and I love pizza rolls!

Noted. See you tomorrow.

I drove to the address sent by Elizabeth this afternoon. The impressive home reminded me of Nana's house and was only a half mile from there. My own home in Naperville had been nice, in a suburban mid-century kind of way, but nothing like these old Southern manors. I almost expected a footman to open my car door and escort me inside.

I rang the doorbell, noticing the camera pointed at my face, so I gave a little wave with my free hand toward it.

When I heard someone approach, I took a final, cleansing breath and pasted on a smile.

The door opened and my father, the dishonorable Judge Arthur Keller, greeted me. "Well, here she is. Right on time. Hello, dear, so glad you could join us. Come in."

"Thanks for the invitation. Something smells fantastic." I was a little nervous, I couldn't lie.

He was dressed in beige slacks, a plaid button-down, and a navy cardigan, and appeared completely at ease bringing me into his family home. "Let's get these opened and breathing." He gently pulled the wine bottles from my tight grasp.

"Your home is lovely." That was an understatement, I realized, but seemed like an appropriate thing to say.

"Tootie, Allison is here." He called toward the staircase and then turned to me. "She's been cooking all afternoon and just went upstairs to freshen up."

"Oh, there you are. Glad you found your way." Elizabeth made her way down the statement staircase and could have been mistaken for a high-fashion model in her gorgeous wrap dress and high heels.

But I refused to cower from my lower position. "Yes, thanks for sending the address."

"Let's go on into the kitchen. I think there's an appetizer or two in there with my name on it." The judge was clearly working to avoid some of the inevitable awkwardness.

He grabbed a corkscrew and began opening the room-temperature red wine. "I'll just put this one in here in the wine fridge so it can chill." He referred to the bottle of chardonnay I'd brought.

"Momma told me to keep an eye on how much bacon

you're eating before dinner, Daddy." Elizabeth said this as they passed through the swinging door into the kitchen.

"I like bacon—a lot—and my latest cholesterol numbers are proof," he said as if it didn't bother him in the least. "The women in my life like to boss me around."

"We don't want you to die from overexposure to pig fat." As a heart surgeon, Elizabeth probably knew what she was talking about.

"I love bacon too," I said, feeling like he could use a little support.

The two appetizer platters sat on the white marble island with barstools set alongside it. This area had been recently renovated—based on the upscale stainless appliances and fixtures. There were cedar beams that ran across the ceiling, which added a less formal appearance than the entrance. I could tell this was a lived-in hub of the home, with its cozy fireplace and keeping area. Someone had done a nice job with the interior decorating here.

"What a great kitchen." It was, and I had nothing else to say now.

"Thanks, Allison." The judge pointed to the finger food. "Have some. We don't get them often, so enjoy."

I picked up a small cocktail napkin and what appeared to be a bacon-wrapped date with a toothpick stuck in it, and then popped it in my mouth. "Mmm. Delicious."

The door swished open, and Mrs. Keller swept through it. "Welcome, Allison. I see these two have led you to the food." The tall woman was stunning with her blond chignon and flowing pantsuit.

I felt underdressed. "Thanks for inviting me over."

She came over to where I sat and took both my hands in hers. "You're Arthur's daughter, which means we are all going to be family. So, let's not allow the town gossip and unflattering talk to get in the way of that." She said this like she'd rehearsed the sweeping statement.

"I appreciate your kind welcome." I tried to sound appreciative, avoiding the dig at the behavior of the folks in town.

Elizabeth held up a wineglass with a generous pour of red as a toast. "Well, I've been an only child for far too long, apparently, so welcome to the family, new sister."

"Thank you, Elizabeth."

The judge patted my hand from his seated position next to me at the bar in front of the bacon treats. "You've got nothing to fear from us, dear. We might seem a little insufferable at times, but we feel it's important to show the community that you're one of us, and that we're proud of you."

Proud of me? I wasn't exactly sure how that message was intended. Were they proud, as in, wanting to embrace me as a family member? Proud, as in, wanting to show me off? Or proud, as in, they'd decided to show this town that they are above the judgment and censure? "Thank you."

"Everybody ready for some gumbo?" Tootie gave the pot a final stir and put a ladle in it.

Gumbo appeared to cure all ills in this town from what I could tell. If someone was sick, they were made better with gumbo and a side of potato salad. I had to admit that Nana's gumbo had worked wonders during my recovery.

We ate at the kitchen table, family style, serving our

plates from the large Dutch oven and a giant bowl of cooked rice. I'd imagined the four of us eating at the ultra-formal dining table that sat at least twelve comfortably. And yes, they were overdressed, but it didn't feel ostentatious. They were fancy people, so I guess this was better than expected so far.

"So, Allison, we'll expect you to join us at least a couple of times a month for a family dinner out. We must show a united front in the community with what's happened to poor Arthur."

Poor Arthur. Got it. I realized that they were putting demands on me to do their bidding, as if my being added to the family was both an honor (for me) and a grave responsibility that required sacrifice (for them). All families required some sacrifice, I realized, but this felt…constructed, maybe? So, proud in this case meant they were going to strategically use my presence to make a statement to the town. Letting the world know that I was officially included and firmly on team Keller. "I'm willing to have dinner with you as long as my schedule allows it."

"We'll of course try to work with your schedule, but you can pretty much depend on alternating Wednesday evenings, starting with cocktails around six o'clock. Maybe that will help with planning your calendar." Tootie expected no guff about it, that was obvious.

"Oh, and we'll host a Christmas party on December twenty-third here at the house for our closest friends and family." Elizabeth supplied this detail.

I wondered if I should pull out my phone and start making notes. Instead, I nodded.

"And we realize that the Bertrand family has helped you a great deal, but I'm sorry to say they aren't our closest friends. There's a lot of dirty water under that bridge, so I hope you understand. And socially, well, we're just not the same."

I didn't precisely know what that meant, or how their poor relationship with my other family affected me. Was I supposed to choose? So, I said, "They've done a lot for me."

Tootie frowned. "Yes, dear. I'm certain they have. Their kind always makes a big show of how united they are. But honestly, after Tanner and Carly worked so hard to take down your *father*, well, obviously there's a conflict of interest there."

That got my back up. *Their kind.* "I'm willing to try and get to know you all, but I won't be forced into choosing one side or the other." I had to show them that I owned a steel spine just like Elizabeth did. Maybe they would respect that at least. If these people thought I would simply cave to their demands, well then, we were going to have a problem.

My show of spine was waved away by Tootie as if I was being silly. "Not choose, precisely. Just show as much support for our family as you do for theirs. You know, Arthur's court date is looming, and we'd like you to sit with the family in support of him." A big family statement for their side, obviously. My skin crawled at the wrongness of it.

I dug in then. "Let's take this slow, okay? I don't know the whole story when it comes to the charges against the judge."

"Well, first thing, stop calling Daddy, *the judge*. Whether any of us likes it or not, we're blood relations. You're his *daughter.*" Elizabeth sounded huffy.

"I don't think I'm quite ready for *Daddy* yet. I'll think about it." With every sentence they uttered, I tightened up. It was like some sort of twisted play where I was expected to perform but hadn't gotten the lines ahead of time.

The judge spoke then. "Well, that's fair enough, dear. I was arrested for helping Carson Carmichael take away poor Marie Trichel's civil liberties. I'd never have considered such a thing if Carson hadn't extorted my support. The two of us go back a long way, since our childhoods, and he's always gotten his way, no matter the cost to others."

"So, are you guilty?" I had to ask, because this had already gone too far, in my opinion. I might as well know all of it.

"Guilt is a harsh word. I made some bad decisions, admittedly, but my involvement pales next to Carson's crimes."

So, he was guilty. Not just of the charges against him, but of being pathetic enough to do what his buddy said, no matter how wrong. I think I would need to shower when I got home to wash off the stench of this entire evening.

Tootie stood and began clearing plates. "Arthur is a good man, Allison, and he's going to need our support. Not everyone in your life will always do the right things. We've had to accept that Carson is his Achilles' heel. Carson has a way about him that makes everyone do his bidding."

"He sounds like a magical creature if everyone does the bad things he suggests, despite them being good people." I'd heard from Carly and Leah that the man had manipulated people all over town for years by holding secrets over their heads they'd not want to get outed for. But it sounded like they'd all thrown their hands up in surrender to him.

"No. Honestly, he's just been an asshole his entire messed-up life." Elizabeth called it what it was, which I could appreciate. "And Daddy's judgment, where Carson is concerned, is shit."

"Bread pudding, anyone?"

CHAPTER TWELVE

I HAD PIZZA rolls, corn dogs, and a big bag of candy corn ready to transport to Nick's house the next day. I was curious about the movie titles I'd texted over. Tonight's outing appeared to be a more promising one than last night.

The dread I'd felt after last night's Keller fiasco had haunted me all day. In fact, I'd not mentioned it to anyone yet, since I was still trying to process all the suggestions that had been made to me. How I should appear at family dinners in public, attend their parties, and make a show of loyalty in court as a devoted puppet, no matter what my true feelings were.

I wondered what the Bertrands thought of these things. They'd not once asked anything of me besides that I give them a chance by living here for a year—which was a different kind of manipulation. But they'd put in the time and work with me so far. The Kellers had not. The Bertrands hadn't suggested outings with the family or public shows of loyalty. And the Kellers had called them, "their kind". A picture was forming fast of how things would be for me here if I didn't continue to stand up for myself. It wasn't a pretty one.

As I headed to Nick's house, I tried to shake off last night's spectacle. Tonight would be fun, so I was determined to ward off the dark cloud of emotions, the evening had stoked.

Another surprise awaited me as I arrived at Nick's "apartment". He'd failed to tell me about the mansion he'd grown up in. My eyes widened at the electronic gate, to which he'd given me the code. He'd said very little other than his was the apartment over the garage at his parents' house. It was quite a nice garage.

The house was stunning. Not historic like some of the ones in town, but it had an established look, a brick ranch with white columns spaced across the front.

I parked in one of the spaces on the concrete parking pad to the side of the four-car garage. By the looks of it, Nick's place over the garage was bigger than mine. As soon as I climbed out of my SUV, Nick jogged up.

"Hey. It's great to see you." His eyes were sincere and, of course, he disarmed me with that gorgeous smile of his.

"Wow. This is a beautiful house."

He spared a quick glance toward the house. "Thanks. So far, I haven't had a good reason to move out."

As he helped me take out the items I'd brought, we heard a woman's voice. "Nick, aren't you going to introduce me to your friend?"

I heard Nick groan and he whispered to me, "I'm sorry about this."

The dark-haired woman who approached them was wearing a pantsuit with a string of pearls and low-heeled pumps. She looked as expensive as Tootie Keller. "I'm Stella Landry."

She held out a hand to shake, but my arms were burdened with items, so I nodded to her. "It's nice to meet you, Mrs. Landry. I'm Allison Miers."

"Of course you are, dear. I can see the family resemblance. Your mother is a great friend, as is your father and his wife, Tootie." She stared at me for another second before adding, "Tootie told me you joined them for dinner last night."

I didn't have an answer for that. This woman claimed to be friends with both branches of my family. The first of her kind that I'd met so far. I got the feeling she wanted me to say more, but Nick intervened. "Mom, we're going upstairs to watch movies. See you later."

"But Allison just arrived. Maybe she'd like a glass of wine and to meet your father."

"She can meet Dad another day. We've got plans tonight." I could tell Mrs. Landry could easily be a bit of a bully, and Nick knew how to handle it, reminding me of my Bertrand sisters and the way they spoke to Karen. It wasn't disrespectful, just straightforward and honest.

"Well, all right. But you must come to dinner one night. I insist." Stella Landry beamed.

"Thank you. I'll look forward to it."

"Night, Mom." Nick took the items from my arms and propelled me toward the garage. Once we were out of earshot, he again apologized.

"Don't worry about it. I understand her…curiosity. And it's the same with almost everyone I've met here."

"Well, I call it rude to ambush you like that. By the way, how was dinner with the Kellers?" We climbed the stairs to his apartment.

"Oh, we'll need some wine before I get into that story."

He laughed and opened the door for me, and my mouth dropped. It was every bit as nice as my apartment. The décor was a bit more masculine, with a large brown leather sectional taking center stage. And the size of the TV was…impressive. The living room rug was a black-and-white print and there were a pair of lamps with bubbled glass on the sofa table behind the sectional.

"Wow, Nick. I can see why you don't move out. This is nice."

"My mother insisted on having her decorator come in and fix it up. I've lived here since starting my second year at NSU. I stayed in the dorms my freshman year, but instead of moving into an apartment after that, I decided to move in here. It was much nicer than the off-campus apartments. Plus, I was tired of roommates."

He turned on the oven to keep the pizza rolls warm. I brought them over in the same pan I'd cook them. Before he popped them in, Nick peeked under the foil. "Hmm. Pizza rolls. Thanks."

"Corkscrew?" I held up the bottle of red wine.

"In the drawer beside the fridge."

While we worked together to get our snacks and drinks in order, he streamed some top-forty tunes on the TV. "I wasn't sure what kind of music you liked."

"My tastes are eclectic. I love country music, pop, and eighties hair band music. And maybe a little classical baroque."

"Glad I didn't try to guess."

"Beer or wine?" I asked.

"Beer."

I pulled out a pale lager from the fridge and noticed how organized the items inside were. No wonder he didn't want messy roommates. "So, what did you think of my movie choices?" I asked.

He laughed. "Nope. Not until you tell me what happened last night at the Kellers' welcome meal. I mean if you want to share." He grabbed a couple of paper plates, and we loaded our snacks onto them.

I took a sip of my wine and perched on one of the barstools. "Let's just say, they had an agenda in bringing me there."

"Not surprised. Were they nasty to you?"

"No. Not exactly. It was more like they gave me the 411 on what their expectations were on my joining the family."

Nick frowned. "Like what?"

"Family dinners twice a month on Wednesdays, the annual Christmas party, and it was strongly suggested that I show up and take sides for the judge's trial by sitting with them."

He grimaced. "Ouch. Backing the judge must be a hard call, huh?" Nick understood the conflict of interest there, thankfully.

"Yes. They also warned me to not be so chummy with the Bertrands."

"I know the Kellers. All of them, and they'll continue to bully you unless you put your foot down from the beginning."

"I did, but of course Tootie waved away my strong stand as if I'd not even spoken. I don't know that I want anything to do with them after last night." I reflected on what an awkward position they'd put me in.

"I don't blame you one bit."

I sighed loudly. "This is all a lot more complicated than I'd anticipated."

"Just make sure to do what you want and don't try and please any of them, the Bertrands included. I know they can be…a lot."

"Yes, they can, but at least they don't tell me what to do or not to do, like the Kellers are trying to."

Nick stood with his beer and plate in hand, moved toward the sofa, and motioned for me to do the same. "We're going to enjoy our evening, starting right now. It's going to be tight with all the movies we've got to watch. I'll admit that your movie choices surprised me. I mean, *Beetlejuice* and *Hocus Pocus*? I'd expected some scarier stuff."

"I like some scary stuff, but I prefer weird and creepy over a bloody slasher." We settled in on the sectional, seated about two feet apart, resting our plates on the coffee table in front of us. Just as Nick switched from music to the home screen for the streaming service, a large dog came bounding into the living room and jumped on the sofa between us, almost knocking my red wine from my hand. "Ooh. Hello there."

"Easy, Buddy." Nick crooned to the animal. "He's not used to having company." Buddy licked my nose, and I laughed.

"Hey, Buddy. Where did you come from, boy?" I asked the dog, whose face was graying. I could tell he was a senior, with those big hound dog eyes staring at me. I scratched the space between his ears, and he immediately plopped down on the sofa, his head on my lap.

"He goes back and forth between here and my parents' house. I've had him since he was a puppy. Some days the stairs are tough for him."

"I'm glad he's having a good day."

Nick smiled at his pup. "Yeah, me too." He grabbed the remote and asked me, "What should we watch first?"

"Let's start out with a little creepy and move to more creepy," I suggested.

"Sounds good. *Hocus Pocus* it is." Nick turned on the movie and we settled in with our snacks.

It was the tale of three witches who'd been unintentionally resurrected by a young boy. Gruesome but funny. We laughed our way through the ninety's classic.

"That one always puts me in the creepy movie mood."

"All righty then, let's move on to *Beetlejuice*." Tonight, I was safe with Nick, so I wanted to enjoy our evening. I noticed that Buddy had moved over to a fluffy dog bed during our conversation and was already snoozing away. The space between Nick and me seemed less now, our thighs nearly touching as we'd both gravitated toward the center during our conversation. I shivered slightly, not from fear, but from excitement.

Nick turned toward me. "Are you cold?"

"Just my hands," I said, rubbing them together for effect, so he didn't suspect the real reason for my shiver: my secret little thrill of sitting so close to him that I could feel his body heat radiating next to me. Before I knew it, he'd pulled my left hand into his, holding it gently and rubbing it between his big, calloused hands to warm me.

Good thing I hadn't lied. My hands *were* a little cold. Nick folded my fingers into his as he used his other one to work the remote control. We sat there, almost snuggling, as we watched our next movie selection.

I felt like a junior high girl sitting there on the sofa beside Nick, holding hands and barely touching. It was a thrill unlike any I'd ever experienced with anyone else as an adult. Our chemistry sizzled, but he didn't make a move, for which I was thankful, because I wasn't feeling like pushing him away. And I couldn't afford to make a mistake with a man I barely knew. Could I?

CHAPTER THIRTEEN

THE NEXT MORNING, I was scheduled to work at eight o'clock, and I was still a little sleepy from my late night out with Nick. We'd had a great time scrutinizing the spooky movies and their plots and it had been well after midnight when I'd gotten home.

Nick had insisted on following me in his truck to make sure I arrived and got inside safely. It seemed like a very old-fashioned thing to do, but it charmed me.

Today, I was busy mass-producing the garland swags Lydia and I had designed together. They'd been immediately approved by her contact at city hall, so Lydia had gone after work to Shreveport to buy the supplies we needed at the wholesale floral mart, which was now staying open later due to the holiday demand.

Since Shreveport was only an hour away from Cypress Bayou, it made good sense to drive the short trip instead of ordering the items and having them shipped. Even if Lydia expedited them, it would've taken at least a couple of days for everything to come in.

"How was your evening?" Lydia asked.

"It was fun. Nick and I had a scary movie marathon at his place." I'd begun to relax around my employer and was able to answer her questions without feeling like she was mining for information about me.

Lydia raised her brows and smiled. "Sounds like you and Nick are an item."

While the idea secretly thrilled me, nothing had happened between us besides a little flirting. "He's been a great friend to me since I moved here."

"He's a nice guy for sure. I don't think I've ever heard anything bad said about him, which is something for around here," Lydia said.

It was good to know that everyone I'd met so far liked Nick. It helped with my confidence in judgment, which had been a little shaky lately.

"Did you do anything fun last night?" I asked Lydia, trying to be polite.

"My husband, Greg, and I went out for an early dinner at The Marina. He loves that place."

"Nick took me there a few nights ago. It was quite good." I didn't mean to mention Nick again, but he was the only person I'd spent time with lately.

"Nick again, huh?" She grinned knowingly as we continued working on the swags.

I shrugged and smiled. "He's been a good friend."

We worked together in comfortable silence until lunchtime. My stomach growled loudly, and I blushed. "Sorry, I ran out without breakfast this morning."

"Oh, honey. You should always eat. Nutrition is important, especially for you, having had cancer and all." Lydia was *momming* me now, but I had to admit I didn't hate it that she was so kind.

I smiled at her. "Yes, you're right." I tidied up my workspace and headed over for some gumbo and a salad down the block.

As I waited for my order in front of the counter, a man around my age in a business suit asked, "Oh, hi. Aren't you Leah and Carly's sister?"

I tried not to sigh aloud at the guy's obvious curiosity. "Yes, that's right."

"It's so nice to meet you. I'm the district attorney here in Cypress Bayou. Alan Litrell." He held out a hand for me to shake, and I did. We made eye contact, and I could appreciate his twinkling brown eyes.

I nearly snatched my bag of food from the guy behind the counter the second he called my name. "It was nice meeting you, Mr. Litrell." I couldn't tell if he was hitting on me or just being friendly. I'd noticed there were a lot of "friendly" folks here, both men and women.

"Alan, please."

Meeting new men made my face flush, and I hated that I wasn't less awkward. Hopefully, I'd not see the district attorney again in any legal capacity, or otherwise.

I WAS SCHEDULED to meet with Carly at her office today after work and sign some paperwork for the trust fund Nana was settling on me. Officially, it was Tanner's law office, but she'd helped him get the business running after she'd finished law school and moved back to Cypress Bayou. Tanner had offered her a job with him when he'd quit at his father's law practice. He'd worked there for several years after law school before going into business for himself, though from what I'd heard, working for Carson Carmichael had been awful.

I'd already gone back to Illinois when Carly moved back home, so I didn't get to spend much time with her while I was here before like I had with Leah, who'd lived in town. But Carly had continued to check in on me, even though we hardly knew each other.

I parallel parked on the curb a few spaces down from the office, fed the meter, and walked the short distance to the front door. There was a camera doorbell, which buzzed almost as soon as I pressed it.

I opened the door and entered the small waiting area. There was an older woman sitting behind a desk. "Hello there, Allison. I'm Imogene. It's so nice to finally meet you. Can I get you some coffee or tea? Water maybe?"

I smiled at the friendly, and obviously helpful woman. "It's nice to meet you. I don't need anything right now, thanks."

"Carly is finishing up a call and will be out momentarily."

"Thanks."

Before I'd had the chance to sit down, Tanner appeared from the back of the office, shrinking the space by half. "Hey there, Allison. Come on back and we'll get settled in the conference room while Carly finishes up on the phone."

"Oh, okay." I followed him down the hall as he led me into a doorway on the right. It was a nice conference room, complete with a large table and chairs, and some lovely paintings on the wall.

He motioned to one of the chairs. "Please make yourself comfortable."

I sat. "Thanks for seeing me this afternoon."

"Of course."

Carly entered the room then. "Hi, Allison. Sorry I got hung up on a call with our mother." She rolled her eyes, as both my sisters often did when Karen's name came up.

"Is she okay?" I asked.

"Depends on who you ask. I'd say she's fine, but according to her, she's dying of neglect since she hasn't seen any of us since dinner last week."

I had to giggle at that. "I'll call her tonight and say hello."

"Do *not* let her drag you to church to meet his holiness, Father Felix. He's a nice man but Mom believes he's the precursor to the second coming."

"Got it." I figured having a sense of humor about this might be the best way to proceed. I would follow the example of my two sisters when it came to Karen and her skewed beliefs. Not that I had a problem with church. It was the level of church that Karen involved herself in.

"So, I suggested this appointment because Nana wanted you to have some money to live on while you're here," Carly said.

"That's kind of her, but I should be okay since I'm working and still have my mom's house settlement." Taking anything from the Bertrands was hard for me, but I'd been read the riot act by Nana about pride.

"I'm glad to hear you've got that, but it's Nana's money and she wants you to have some of it now in case there's something you want or need."

"Well, I appreciate it." I didn't ask for it, but I did appreciate it.

"Isn't there anything you want to do? I mean, you're a cancer survivor and have an amazing opportunity to do anything you want with your life now."

I thought about that for a second. Before my mom got sick, I was dead set on my dream of starting my own interiors and accessories business. "I've got a few ideas, but nothing I can really pursue unless I decide to stay here permanently." I didn't want to put anything out there yet to my family. This was my dream and it felt very private and personal.

"Well, we're here to help. As you can tell, our family has a lot of pent-up guilt over the way Momma handled things back then. With you."

"Well, I have to admit that my intentions weren't the best when I set out to find my family. I was angry and wanted to shame them. It wasn't about being given away; it was more about not allowing contact once I was older. But I met you all and well, I couldn't do it."

"Thank goodness for the bone marrow registry. Obviously we weren't there when you were born, so trying to go back isn't possible. Momma was obsessed with what the town would think of her delivering a baby out of wedlock and going against such a powerful family like the Kellers…well, let's just say that the judge is a picnic in the park compared to his father."

"The senior Judge Keller died twenty years ago, but he would've fought to the death to run Karen and Nana out of town if she'd called Arthur out publicly as being your father," Tanner added. "The situation must've been a nightmare for both Nana and Karen. I'm not saying it was right, but the consequences were heavily stacked in the Kellers' favor."

"Men using their power to cow women. It's an age-old story." Carly shook her head sadly.

"I guess it could've turned out worse. You all could have rejected me to save Karen's reputation in Cypress Bayou."

"There's no way that would've happened, Allison, and I hope you realize how sorry Momma and Nana are for how this has all gone."

"I've forgiven them. But sometimes I'm not sure what they did was right."

"Agreed. So, enjoy the money and don't hesitate to lean on the family for anything. And let us know if you need anything."

I thought of something I'd been meaning to ask. "Do you know if there's a key to the metal gate at the apartment?"

"I'll find out who has the key. It's either with Jake and Leah still, or Mrs. Sibley," Tanner said.

"I can't thank you both enough. I'm not sure what I would've done without your help." I could feel my eyes tearing a little, so I blinked away the moisture. I didn't want to seem weak.

Carly covered my hand with hers, and I noticed that our hands were similar with long fingers and deep nail beds. Funny how DNA did that. "Honey, we're going to make sure you're not alone. Promise you'll call us anytime for any reason." I suddenly felt like the little sister instead of nearly a decade her senior. Our eyes met and I felt a kinship pass between our gazes.

"I promise."

"Hey, why don't you join us for dinner tonight? We're heading out after work for some Italian food as soon as we're done. You're our last appointment of the day," Carly suggested.

The idea of having dinner with my youngest sister gave me a warm feeling, and it meant I didn't have the entire evening to fill alone. I could only ask so much of Nick, and since we'd been together last night, I didn't want to impose on him. "That sounds nice."

"We're going to The Garden on Washington Street. Their veal parmigiana is to die for."

"I'm looking forward to eating so much garlic, Carly won't kiss me for week." Tanner grinned.

"The whole trailer will smell like it for at least two days, but it's worth it." Carly gave him a playful punch in the arm.

"Okay, I'll meet you there. I'll stop by my place and change."

"No need. It's totally casual, like most places around here. When you live in a college town, there isn't a lot of dressing up."

"Except the Kellers. They put on the dog whenever they go out, just FYI. They make the rounds to all the nicer restaurants in town wearing their church clothes." Tanner stated this truth that I'd already figured out.

I laughed. "I had dinner at their house a few days ago and I thought they were dressed pretty fancy for a dinner at home." The words "church clothes" cracked me up. It sounded so Southern to my Midwestern ears.

"Oh, that's right. Elizabeth mentioned it to Jake at the hospital the other day, and Jake told us. I've been dying to find out how that went." Carly shared this bit of gossip about my comings and goings without blinking. "We can talk about how it went at dinner."

NICK MET UP with his usual group of friends and helped them light up an enormous Santa with numerous strings of red and clear lights.

"Did you ask Allison if she wanted to come out here today?" Savannah asked.

He shook his head. "She's got something going on after work or she would've been here." Allison had texted him to let him know that she was meeting with Carly and Tanner when she got off work.

"My mom says she's got a great eye. Says she's creative as hell and fast as lightning. And you know Lydia doesn't sing many people's praises," Kimmie said.

"I had a feeling they were hitting it off." Nick felt an unexpected surge of pride on Allison's behalf that Mrs. Donovan was happy with her work at her shop.

"Sounds like she's just the *best*, huh?" Izzy chimed in, her tone sarcastic, as she uncoiled a long strand of lights.

"Now, Izzy. You need to drop the attitude about Allison. She's super nice and doesn't deserve that kind of treatment." Kimmie stuck up for their new friend to their old friend. "You and Nick aren't together, so let it go." Her words were a little harsh, but Nick knew Kimmie felt it was time for Izzy to stop hanging any hope on him. He hadn't had the heart to be so direct with her.

Izzy narrowed her eyes at Kimmie, then threw a glance over at Nick. "You just met her and you're taking her side?"

"Side? There's no side, honey. It's just time for you to let it go." Kimmie laid a hand on Izzy's shoulder. The two women had been friends since kindergarten.

Nick appreciated Kimmie's support of Allison but hated that her words hurt Izzy. He didn't hold any hard feelings against her. They'd dated in their teens mostly, and the spark wasn't there for him as adults. She'd carried a torch for Nick all these years and he wished there was something he could say to make her feel better.

Izzy narrowed her eyes at Kimmie.

Nick decided it was time to weigh in. "Listen, Izzy, I don't want y'all to fight about Allison. And I don't want you to get hurt feelings about her. You and I haven't dated in years. I thought we were friends."

Izzy shrugged a shoulder. "I get a little pissy when somebody else tries to worm their way into our group. And yes, it bothers me that you have eyes for her." At least Izzy was honest, he'd give her that. "Don't worry, Nick. I'll be nice. It's my problem to deal with."

"Thank you."

Glad to have that conversation over with, he quickly changed the subject. "All right, gang, let's get this Santa lit." They had a lot to do in a short amount of time to get this piece lit up like the others popping up along the bank of the bayou. "How many surge suppressors do y'all think we're going to need for this one?"

"So, are you planning to invite Allison to join our group tomorrow?" They'd all volunteered through the city council to help do the lighting on three more pieces.

"Yes. I'm planning to. But listen, I haven't told Allison anything about myself besides that I'm a dirty mechanic and I kind of like it." He grinned at his oldest friends.

They all nodded, but Kimmie spoke up. "Okay, but don't you think you should come clean with her that you run things? I mean, you seem to like her, and she's bound to find out soon enough in this town. If I were Allison, I'd think you were playing games with my head."

"Maybe so. But she's got a lot of personal stuff going on right now, and I'll find the right time to tell her. I just don't want her to find out until I'm ready."

"Your call, dude. But I'm with Kimmie on this one," Jack said. "It's widely known now that you're the boss. I mean, won't the Bertrands tell her?"

"They haven't yet. I'll tell her soon."

Of course, anyone could spill the beans to Allison since it wasn't really a secret here. Any of her family, at any time, so he'd need to tell her soon all about himself. After all, they knew the auto shops were his family's business, and they knew he'd gotten a postgraduate degree—he was sure of it.

CHAPTER FOURTEEN

I ARRIVED AT the restaurant at the same time as Carly and Tanner, so we were able to walk in together. There was no wait this early in the evening, so the host showed us to a booth immediately. "Hmm. It smells so good. Like garlic and cheese." I inhaled deeply, appreciating the aroma.

"Just wait. They bring you garlic yeast rolls sprinkled with obscene amounts of Parmesan." Carly put a hand to her abdomen. "I've just talked my stomach into growling."

The place was small with lanterns on the wall at every booth. There were tables covered with red-and-white checked tablecloths for larger parties in the center of the room.

Carly and I ordered a glass of chardonnay, and Tanner got a beer. "So, I was thinking that we should install some security cameras at street level and outside your door upstairs for peace of mind," Tanner said and took a swig of his beer.

"Is there a crime problem in the area?"

"No, there isn't, but we would feel better with you living alone there if you had a little security."

That was reasonable. Living in the Chicago area, even a nice suburb, I took precautions. "Okay. Thanks for your concern over my safety."

Carly leaned in. "So, I'd love to hear about your dinner

with the Kellers, if you want to talk about it."

"How many hours do you have?" I laughed. "No, I'm kidding. It was an interesting meal for sure. The food was good, and I was welcomed into the family with Tootie listing all the things expected of me as such."

"Oh, dear. I can only imagine. Were you given a list of key words and phrases to embrace or avoid?"

"Ha. No, but there are expectations. They want me to sit with them in the courtroom as a show of support when the judge goes on trial." I knew how sensitive this subject might be, but better to put it out there than keep secrets. I hated secrets.

Tanner's expression became thunderous. "Of all the disgusting things I expected, that's beyond the pale. Do you *know* what he did?"

"I've heard a version of it."

"My father, Carson, was the mastermind, but the judge was nowhere near innocent or blameless. He sat on the bench and signed off on committing a woman to a mental institution to hide the truth about what happened to her daughter back when they were in law school. They hid damning evidence of their involvement to save themselves."

"Wow."

Carly added, "Suffice to say, the judge doesn't deserve your support, but that's for you to decide." But I didn't get the impression they would be okay if I decided to show support for the judge.

"The Bertrands have been there for me since the day you found out about me. But I've barely spoken to the Kellers. I can't help but feel they're playing me to help their situation in the community—or something."

"They are a calculating bunch. Elizabeth despises Leah because she's had a thing for Jake since they were kids. Mom hates Arthur Keller and Carson for threatening her when she got pregnant with you. She blames them both for your adoption."

Every time somebody mentioned my adoption, I got a hard kick in the gut. "Yes, Karen gave a me a short version of it." I didn't want to go there right now since Carly was so fired up, so I focused on the bad blood between my two sisters. "I've heard about *Team Leah* from Nick's friends. People do like to talk about our families."

"It's a real thing. I guarantee that *Team Leah* has a lot more members than *Team Elizabeth*." I could hear the censure in Carly's tone.

"I've yet to hear anyone say something nice about Elizabeth. She doesn't make a great first impression, that's for sure." I pictured Elizabeth at the café, tapping her foot with impatience.

"Our families don't get along for many reasons. Those are just a couple of them. Now they're trying to put you publicly on their side."

Sidestepping, I asked, "So, Tanner and Jake's dad had an unholy alliance with the judge from their teenage years, through law school, and even now?"

"Unholy is a good word for their friendship and business agreements. They kept each other's damaging secrets all those years," Tanner said. "You never get used to having a father who is scum. We worked for months with the DA to take them down for their crimes."

At the mention of the DA, I said, "I met the DA when I ran out to pick up lunch at the café near Donovan's. He seemed nice." I was curious to hear their thoughts.

"Yes, Alan's a great guy. His wife is pregnant with their first child," Tanner said.

"Ah. That's nice." So that answered my question about whether he was hitting on me. I would need to adjust my social expectations about people here. I guessed it might be because strangers weren't as overtly friendly from where I came. Very rarely did people strike up conversations with strangers getting takeout.

"He was instrumental in nailing those two—finally."

I considered that. Was the judge actual scum or was there anything redeemable about him? I realized that the Bertrands had very specific reasons to despise him, and it would be up to me if I decided to give him a chance to be a part of my life. The man had seemed amicable enough to me, so I couldn't say anything about his demeanor.

I felt like I was being pulled apart between my two birth families, though I certainly leaned toward my mother's side. If I stayed in Cypress Bayou, would it ever end?

Changing the subject yet again, I asked, "So where's a good place to get a new phone? Mine is getting a little glitchy."

"Depends on who your carrier is, or you might want to change carriers altogether, depending on your contract. You can use Radio Shack or Walmart, or there's a Verizon store and an AT&T dealer an hour and a half away in Shreveport."

I'd flown into Shreveport last summer when I came for

Karen and Bob's ceremony. Leah had picked me up from the airport and brought me straight to Cypress Bayou, so I wasn't exactly familiar with the city.

The food arrived then and we dug in. The rolls and chicken parm were indeed manna from heaven, and I savored every garlicky bite. "Looks like we won't need any to-go boxes tonight." The waistband of my jeans was uncomfortably tight.

I felt my phone vibrate in my purse next to me. I hesitated to check it, but I pulled it up and glanced at the screen. I blew out a relieved breath because it was from Nick.

The evening ended with Tanner and Carly following me home to make sure I got inside okay. Not only did I have a new family, but now they were acting like the secret service. I appreciated their concern, but I felt like a child being followed around.

Hi there. Just checking in on you.

I responded to Nick's text once I got home from dinner. *I'm home now. Had dinner with Carly and Tanner.*

I jumped a little when my phone rang. It was Nick. "Hi."

We chatted for a couple of minutes about our days, and I mentioned Tanner's suggestion about the security cameras. "I'll be happy to help Tanner with the cameras. I installed them inside and out at the garage last year after we had a couple cars broken in to on our lot. Luckily, it turned out to be local kids, but it's nice having the option to take a quick look that everything is as it should be."

"Thanks for offering. I'll speak with Tanner and find out what his plans are for installation. I'm not sure if he'll hire someone or do it himself." I briefly wondered why Nick would install the cameras at the garage. He appeared to be a very valuable employee.

"We're getting together on the bayou tomorrow to string lights after work if you'd like to join us. Izzy promised to be nice."

"Oh, did you discuss me?" His mention of Izzy got my attention.

"We did, but the real discussion was long overdue between us. I'd kind of allowed her jealous behavior so as not to hurt her feelings. Let's face it; it's been years since Izzy and I dated, but Kimmie was the one who laid it out to her. Everybody likes you, and it's not fair for Izzy to behave in ways that make you uncomfortable."

"I honestly don't want to cause any trouble between you and your lifelong friends. I mean, who knows if I'll even be here a year from now." I was thinking out loud and realized that Nick had gotten quiet.

"I hope that you will." His tone was serious.

"But this town. I haven't made up my mind about it yet. I agreed to give the Bertrands a year, so I'll stick to that." I'd decided I couldn't be the pleaser I'd always been. It was time to do what was best for me. I was in a unique position to do that since I didn't have any real attachments or obligations currently.

"I get it that Cypress Bayou is like something out *Sweet Home Alabama*, but please keep your mind open to the good things about it—and its people."

"I promise, and I hope you don't take my reservations about the place personally. How do you feel about heading to Shreveport with me to phone-shop one evening this week or on the weekend? Mine is getting old and is starting to act up."

"I'd be honored. How about Thursday evening after work?"

"Thanks. I don't know my way around Shreveport, and I figured you likely do."

"I sure do. Been making trips there my whole life for all the things we can't get here."

We hung up after discussing tomorrow's meeting time and location, and I promised Nick that I would lock up tight.

But even as I thought this, I could see the faces of Nick, my sisters, Nana, and yes, Karen, and experienced a little guilt. *Were they finding their way into my life and maybe my heart just a little?* That wasn't something I'd expected.

NICK GOT A call late that night from an employee informing him that there'd been a fire at the shop down in Lafayette—fortunately, nobody was hurt. It wasn't a complete loss, but it was his job to deal with the insurance adjuster, schedule repairs and order new equipment, and manage the employees who would need to take some time off while the garage was being fixed.

He hated to leave town now because of the relationship

he was forming with Allison, but this was an emergency. Nick still hadn't come clean with her about his role in the family business, or that the shop was part of the larger family business. Or that there even was a family business. He'd allowed her to believe he was a hired mechanic.

Growing up in the Deep South, racism was a real thing, though Allison hadn't seemed to care that he was Creole. There were lots of Creole people indigenous to the Cypress Bayou area and beyond, so it wasn't that he felt out of place. He was like so many others; his dad was half Creole and him mom was white. There'd been so many instances throughout his lifetime—reminders that he was somehow "less" due to being browner than most of his friends—that made him pause before blindly trusting romantic interests.

Making women prove themselves was kind of a thing with him. Admittedly, it was ill-mannered behavior, but he'd had a few gold-digger experiences, unfortunately, causing Nick to carry a considerable chip on his shoulder about how women treated him until they knew he was educated and his family was somewhat wealthy. This usually happened outside of Cypress Bayou or with someone new in town since everybody here knew him and knew his family.

While he understood prejudice against his blue-collar lifestyle, it was important that someone love him for him and not his family's money. Of course, Allison had seen his parents' home, but she hadn't asked any questions about his family's obvious means. It might've seemed strange to her that he still lived above his parents' garage at his age, but she hadn't acted like it was a peculiar thing.

He only hoped she didn't learn something that made him look like a liar while he was away. Allison was someone he could get serious about and losing the chance with her before he'd gotten the opportunity to try was causing him to worry a little. Usually, he wasn't the anxious type, but he didn't want to screw this up.

At three a.m., it was too late—more like too early—to send Allison a text. He didn't want to wake her. He could call her later and explain that he'd gone out of town.

He felt stupid allowing things to go this far with Allison without coming clean about his dual occupation. Maybe she wouldn't care at all, but he'd gotten the vibe from her that truth was important. More than money. She'd been burned by misinformation her entire life, it seemed.

Allison had been given up for adoption as an infant, and while her adoptive parents sounded almost perfect, Nick had absorbed her loneliness and confusion when it came to family. He understood the isolation of being an only child but could only imagine the abandonment of being given away to another family, no matter how great they were.

As he packed his overnight bag, he added a few more clothes. Hopefully, he would only be gone a couple days, but he wouldn't know until he arrived and personally evaluated the situation. They were fully insured, but the loss of business while the shop closed for repairs all hit the bottom line in the end. And he was still trying to prove himself to his parents so they would feel confident in his ability to run ten auto shops and still work on cars most days.

Nick's parents and employees were depending on him to get things up and running quickly.

He would miss seeing Allison, and wished she already knew about his job situation, but a few more days wouldn't likely hurt anything.

CHAPTER FIFTEEN

At seven o'clock, my eyes popped open. I had to be at work by eight, so even though I'd forgotten to set my alarm, there was plenty of time. After a quick shower, I dressed hurriedly and made a quick cup of coffee.

As I was locking the door, I heard a text come through. It was from Nick's number.

Hi there. I've been called down to Lafayette for a few days to help with some car stuff. I'll keep in touch about our trip to Shreveport later in the week.

I raised my brows, wondering what kind of *car stuff* had him leaving town so last minute. But I understood that we weren't at the stage where I had any reason to expect more than that, or to question him beyond what his text said. If he wanted me to know, he would tell me more later.

Okay. I'll see you when you get back. Be safe. Since we'd met, he hadn't left town for any reason.

The temperature was brisk on this Tuesday, maybe low forties, which was walking weather where I came from. I noticed a few people out early in their heavy coats. I wore a sweater and a light jacket. Admittedly, I was a little chilly when the wind blew, but this was nothing like the single-digit temps that Chicago and the surrounding area were having right now.

I still checked the weather back home on my phone app. It was a habit, and it meant keeping a little piece of who I was. I'd lost my identity when I found my family here. Learning that I was born in the deepest south had been a real kicker. Where I grew up, the general consensus about people who lived below the Mason-Dixon Line wasn't especially favorable.

Stereotypes were unfair since people were individuals, not the groups they represented. It was a decidedly different culture here and coming from a place where accents and attitudes were dissimilar, I tried not to judge and to separate assumptions from truths with everyone I met. There were people here who'd honestly impressed me, despite the twang and added syllables in their speech, causing words to hang on their lips. There was a relaxed, friendly vibe here in Cypress Bayou, for the most part. Sometimes too friendly, but I was learning to be patient. Here, strangers said hello or smiled in greeting when I walked to and from work. In Chicago, people mostly looked down, often due to the cold and a quicker pace, and minded their business.

So, I was still tallying up the plusses and minuses in my mind. Stay and make a life here? Or go back to what was familiar, albeit lonely? My perception was ever-changing based on my daily experiences. I was just as confused now as I'd been when I'd set out on this journey.

I arrived at work ready to dive into whatever Lydia had planned for me today. The bells jingled, as always when I entered. Lydia greeted me. "Hey there, Allison. I've put some orders at your workstation. If you have any questions, let me know." She appeared to be lost in a pile of paperwork.

"Great. I'll get started."

The orders were straightforward, so I spent the morning doing mostly poinsettia centerpieces, modeled from what Lydia had shown me. I'd looked up the Donovan's website one evening out of curiosity and noticed that Lydia took orders online from her website. There were several seasonal offerings at reasonable prices, including the poinsettia centerpiece. All one had to do was add it to the cart and pay with any number of optional methods.

The process was streamlined and efficient. We filled those orders, and the customers came and picked them up, unless they required a larger install. Lydia had workers who she contracted to decorate Christmas trees and others who put up lights on homes and do the exterior yard décor. So far, I'd worked only in the shop. "You could open your own business, you know?" I looked up from my work to see Lydia watching me. "I mean, I'm not telling you to go out and be my competition, but honey, you've got a gift. Things seem to spring to life while you work. I feel like this is simple busy work for you."

I smiled, a whoosh of excitement at the thought of it. "Thanks. I have so many ideas, and I'd given it some thought before I left Chicago, but a lot has happened since then. Plus, I'm not sure I'm going to stay here long term."

"Well, I prefer selling furniture and decorating people's homes to making anything. But there's not another business doing artificial arrangements here in town, besides the florists, and they prefer to stick with mostly fresh flowers and greenery besides grave arrangements. It would be a niche market if you opened an accessory shop for the public and as a supplier for people like me. You'd stay busy, I'm sure of it."

"Hmm. I'll give it some thought. Mrs. Sibley, my landlord, said she'd make the old soap store available if I ever considered doing something with it."

"Yes, it's hard to see that space sitting empty right on Front Street. Such a prime location and Mrs. Sibley has it locked down tight, from what I hear. Won't rent it to anyone, or not so far. She's funny like that." Lydia's words didn't seem critical of Mrs. Sibley, just that she was eccentric, which I'd already learned.

The conversation with Lydia played through my mind over and over as I worked. It could be the opportunity I should take advantage of. But I had a great fear of failing. Not just with a business, but with all the new people in my life. With Nick, maybe?

I entered the café down the street at lunchtime and nearly walked right into my sister Elizabeth. She was already there when I entered, so I guess she wasn't stalking me. "Hi." I greeted her in line from a couple spots back when our eyes met.

She turned and gave me a tight smile. "Oh, hi. I didn't expect to see you here."

"I work just down the way, so it's a convenient lunch spot." We made small talk as I ordered, and she waited for her food.

She pulled up that expensive watch to check the time. "I guess we could have lunch together if you have time." Somehow it sounded like she'd be doing me a favor.

I had time but I wasn't at all sure if I wanted to have lunch with Elizabeth. I thought about it for a second and realized that it might be my sister's way of extending an olive branch. "I've got almost an hour."

"Meet me outside. It's too stuffy in here." She was right about that. The charming café was filled with the lunch crowd. There were a few tables where people were eating, but the rest of the place was packed.

I nodded my agreement. I grabbed the to-go bag when my number was called and headed outside, where the weather was surprisingly nice, despite the cool temps. "Over here." Elizabeth called out to me from where she was sitting at a small bistro table on the sidewalk outside the restaurant. "I caught somebody leaving and grabbed their table." The table was in the sun, so thankfully, we weren't cold.

"That was lucky." There were several other tables outside, but none were currently available.

Elizabeth pulled a sandwich wrapped in butcher paper out of the bag and began to unwrap it. "I'm starving. I started surgery at six this morning."

I opened my Styrofoam container and inhaled. "Ah. Smells so good." I'd developed a real love for shrimp gumbo, so I'd gotten it with a side of potato salad.

"I hope you're watching your cholesterol. Folks move to Louisiana and the first lab test that goes up is lipids because of all the shrimp and shellfish they consume."

"Hmm. I hadn't thought of that. I've never had high cholesterol, but I heard the judge mention it. I hadn't thought about the cholesterol from seafood. When I was recovering from cancer, they did tons of blood work."

"If you eat most of your calories as red meat, fried food, or seafood, you end up with a significant problem." She snorted. "Daddy hasn't ever been one to abstain from his favorite foods."

"Does it run in the family?" I asked, realizing that these were the kinds of things I should find out. I hadn't thought of her as actually doing heart surgery or as a doctor, and it gave me a bit of perspective.

"I don't think so. So far, mine has been fine." She took a sip from her water bottle. "Next time, come to my office for your labs. We've got great phlebotomists, and we take most insurance plans."

"I need to look into new medical insurance since my coverage from the bone marrow matching service will run out soon." I was glad she'd reminded me of it, but the idea that my cancer might come back was something I didn't allow myself to dwell on. "Thanks for that. Here's hoping it doesn't come back."

"Well, I won't charge you until we can file insurance, and I imagine Jake wouldn't either, but if you have a recurrence, you'll at least need a major medical plan."

"Thanks for bringing it to my attention." I looked down at the yummy potato salad and sighed. My health hadn't been something I'd worried about until cancer. Instead of wallowing in those thoughts, I changed the subject. "What time do you get off?"

"I've got a stent to place after lunch. I'm off after that, probably around three if all goes well." She finished her sandwich, rolled the wrapping, and then placed it inside the bag. "How are you for money?" Elizabeth asked bluntly. "I heard about your nana's trust fund."

I didn't know exactly what she'd heard, so I shrugged

and said, "I'll get the money with the stipulation that I stay in Cypress Bayou for a year. I've got some savings from the sale of my mom's house."

"Well, listen, I'm not hurting any, so if you need money until then, let *me* know. Not Daddy."

I was surprised at her offer. "Thank you, Elizabeth. Hopefully, I won't need any until then."

"Don't be proud, okay?" I saw Elizabeth's eyes soften momentarily. She'd let the force field down for a split second. "We Kellers have a pride gene that can be our downfall."

"That's good to know. I'll let you know if I get stuck." She was being generous, if not kind, so the least I could do was agree to accept help if I needed it.

We stood from the table and threw our trash in the nearest bin. Elizabeth turned and spoke. "Well, I was thinking, since we are sisters, we might as well get to know each other. I realize that I'm not the most popular person in town or with the Bertrands, but I'm willing if you are." It was as close to humble as I'd seen her so far.

"I'm willing to try, and not choose a team." I wondered if she'd get my reference.

"Oh, you've heard about my enmity with Leah, huh? What can I say? We loved the same man for years. Jake and I were close while we were in medical school together. How was I to know he only wanted to be friends? We spent a lot of time together when Leah went off to Paris for those two years. I'll admit I had a hard time when she got back, watching Jake moon over her. I finally understood that he'd never been attracted to me. It was a tough discovery."

We walked across the brick street and sat down together on one of my favorite benches. "I feel so removed from everybody on both sides of my family. I know very little about everyone's past besides some retellings here and there."

"Well, they'll tell you what a raging bitch I am for sure. And I can't say I blame them for their opinion. I've said and done many things I'm not proud of. My people skills aren't the best. I have absolutely no patience for bullshit and that translates to how I'm viewed around here."

"I kind of get that. The entire town believes it knows everything about me, and I've only met a few people here. They lead with: 'Oh, yeah, you're Karen Bertrand's secret baby with the judge.' I feel like I've already been judged or put into a slot. Like I'm not a real person, only what they've decided I am based on what they've heard."

"They are easily entertained, that's for sure. But after growing up here and coming back after college to be near my family, I can honestly say that they're not all bad. I take half the blame at least for my attitude. Maybe I'm not the sweetest personality, but I'm honest about it."

"And you have the best shoes," I joked, making light of both our situations.

Elizabeth laughed out loud, which surprised me. "Maybe you and I aren't so different. I need to take you shopping."

Elizabeth said she'd be in touch soon and left there smiling. It had been an unexpected encounter, but pleasant, nonetheless. I believed I'd created some headway with Elizabeth today.

As I made my way back to the shop, I noticed that the town was turning red and green and twinkly right before my eyes. Nearly every storefront was decorated for the holidays and there were signs out advertising specials for Christmas. The mild weather was strikingly different than every other Christmas I'd celebrated. And I kept thinking about my mom. I was pulled out of my melancholy by my phone vibrating.

It was a text from Nick: *Everything going okay there? I'm sorry to say that I may be gone the rest of the week. I wish I was there to go with you to Shreveport.*

I was sorry to learn this. I would've enjoyed having Nick accompany me to Shreveport for a new phone. But his business was his.

CHAPTER SIXTEEN

I MET UP with Nick's friends after work to help light up a great big wreath with green, red, and clear lights. "Where's Nick?" Jack asked me when I arrived a few minutes later than the others.

"He had to go out of town for a few days, but he didn't say why."

Nobody behaved as if Nick's leaving town was unusual, which felt strange because I was the only one who didn't have a clue.

I'd left Donovan Interiors an hour early to help with the lights. I'd gone in a little early and upped my pace a bit, so we didn't get behind. We strung lights for an hour or so until it got dark. The recent time change meant that it was mostly dark when I left work. Even though it was only a few blocks from my place, walking home in the dark alone probably wasn't such a great idea.

"Do y'all want to grab some dinner?" Kimmie asked the group. "I'm starving."

"I'm headed over to Leah and Jake's place for dinner. I'd love to next time." I'd gotten a text from Leah after I'd returned from lunch. She insisted I come over there when we were done here.

"Can't tonight. We've also got a family dinner," Jack

said, nodding toward Izzy. "Let's plan to do it next week."

As the group split up, I made a beeline to my apartment, heading upstairs and changing into fresh clothes. After a full day's work and an hour outdoors wrestling with Christmas lights, I felt grubby. I brushed my hair, added a light spritz of body spray, and headed out. I'd not been to Carly's, or Leah's houses for that matter since I'd been here. In the span of months, I'd been back in Illinois, Leah and Jake had gotten married and Carly and Tanner had gotten together.

So, Leah's house was begun a few months before Carly's. It was the first family dinner she'd hosted so far, apparently.

I locked my place up tight and turned on the flashlight on my phone to navigate my way downstairs in the dark. Even though I'd flipped the porch light on, it wasn't bright enough to see well once I'd taken a few steps down.

I drove the short distance to Leah and Jake's house, and just before I arrived, I noticed that Carly and Tanner's almost-finished house stood about a quarter of a mile off the street. I could hardly see what it was going to look like because there weren't any lights on. Tanner's Airstream trailer sat only a few feet away, its lights spilling out through the open front door.

Carly came out to greet me as I parked. "Glad you could make it. Leah's pretty excited about the house."

"I can't wait to see it. Nana says it's amazing."

"Well, you know Leah." She waved a hand in a circle. "All that artwork and stuff. And yes, it is amazing."

"I didn't bring anything though." I had a moment's feeling that I'd forgotten something.

I looked toward the significant-sized house, lights ablaze.

It was new, I knew, but it appeared to have all the architectural details of a historic home.

"It's gorgeous. It looks like it's been here as long as Nana's house." It was an Acadian cottage style with a front porch spanning across the front of the house. Every single detail was perfection, from the glossy black storm shutters to the tall, mahogany front door. The outdoor landscape lights illuminated the exterior, so we didn't have any trouble seeing our path.

As we stepped onto the porch, the door swung open, Leah smiling in welcome. "I saw you on the camera."

"Your home is dreamy." I couldn't think of another word.

Leah grinned and then moved to hug me, which, as usual, caught me off guard. "So glad you could make it. I haven't finished decorating yet because the Christmas stuff's going up anyway. I might ask your opinion on it when I'm ready."

"I'd be honored." A little thrill ran through me at the thought of diving into a full-scale house decorating project. Especially, since it was my sister. Carly was right about Leah's artwork. I could see how some great accessories would set it off even more.

We moved inside, through the foyer, past the cozy living room, and finally, into the kitchen, where Jake was stationed at the ginormous eight-burner gas range, wearing a "kiss the cook" apron.

"Hey there, Allison. Great to see you." Jake had been my doctor and cared for me after I'd gotten out of the hospital and during the interim when I'd stayed in Cypress Bayou to get my strength back. So, I felt like I knew him a little better than I did Tanner.

"Hi, Jake. Something smells great."

"It's my super-secret jambalaya. If I tell anyone in this family how I make it, they'll figure out a way to do it better."

"We stay away while he's putting it together and give him his space." Leah laughed, but then threw him an adoring glance, which he returned.

"Don't worry, your secret's safe around me. Cooking isn't my thing."

Jake pulled back in mock horror. "Being a great cook is a main criteria for being a member of this family."

"She'll learn, don't you worry," Carly said, throwing an arm over my shoulders. The physical touching was becoming less unexpected, and I saw it coming this time and managed not to stiffen.

"Love this kitchen," I said to Leah. I noticed all the high-end appliances and could appreciate how well planned the space was. I'd often helped clients with their renovation and building plans to get the most out of their spaces.

"Thanks, Allison. I'm just now getting used to having my own house. I love that we're not always in the same room."

"I'm a little hurt by that, darling," Jake teased. "Except when she's on business calls for the gallery."

We gathered around the large, round table in the kitchen and Jake served his secret jambalaya with a side of red beans and rice and a bowl of green salad with lemon vinaigrette.

"So, Carly, when are you moving into the new house?" I asked, making conversation. Tanner had come in a few minutes ago, just as Jake finished cooking.

"We're hoping to finish everything between Christmas and New Year's. I don't have any interest in moving until after Christmas."

"Don't let her fool you. She's just putting off leaving my trailer." Tanner winked.

"I think you'll actually cry when we move out," Carly teased him.

"It's our home. But worry not, I plan to keep it for future excursions."

Carly rolled her eyes. "I'm not even gonna ask what that means."

They ate and laughed through dinner.

"Oh, Tanner, that reminds me: Nick said he was willing to help install the cameras outside the loft. But he's out of town right now." I didn't want to forget to mention it while I was here.

"I'd be happy for his help. I've already purchased the devices, so anytime in the next few days after work is good for me."

"He was supposed to go to Shreveport with me one day after work to get a new phone, but I'm not sure when he'll be back." I wanted to ask if they knew anything about Nick's travel, but I held back, not wanting to overplay my hand when it came to Nick and me. I was beginning to think we were moving toward a dating relationship, despite my reservations over starting a new relationship so soon—and my doubts about living in Cypress Bayou beyond the one year.

I wanted to be open to new things while I was here and

maybe that could lead me to a real decision about the future. Knowing I would always run the risk of the cancer returning, I could admit that I was scared to be alone if it did, and I didn't have much of a support system now that Mom was gone. But I did love my job there and the charm of my Midwestern hometown. Besides the winters, I would miss it.

"Let me know when he gets back, and if it's more than a few days, I'll come over there and handle it."

"Thanks, Tanner."

"Oh, Allison, I meant to tell you that Lisa said hello. I spoke to her this morning and she's coming to Thanksgiving dinner next week," Leah said.

"Oh, that will be nice. We were supposed to keep in touch after Karen and Bob's vow renewal, but things got away from me." Lisa knew she was adopted, same as me, but had found out that Carson was her real father after hiring Tanner and Carly to help her find out what had happened to her birth mom. So, our situations, while different, were similar in ways that counted.

"From her too, I think. Anyway, she wants the two of you to get together when she's in town. Says she'll call you in a couple of days. I made sure she had your number."

"Great. Is Doug coming with her?" I asked. Lisa's husband was a doctor and often was on call, so frequently unavailable. He and Jake were becoming friends from what I'd heard through the family grapevine. Everybody seemed to like Doug in the family.

"She wasn't sure when we spoke."

"Maybe when Lisa's here I won't feel like the alien in town." I said this without thinking.

"Oh, no. I'm sorry you're feeling that way," Carly said, frowning.

"It's a little better now that people in town have gotten past their initial shock over my arrival. I'm less of a stranger now than I was, maybe."

"They're just fascinated by the stories of both your families. And yes, Lisa will likely get the same treatment. She left town soon after she found out about Carson being her father and has only come back the one time, for the vow renewal," Leah said from across the bar.

"Yes, it's like I'm a character in some movie. No offense to you all."

Leah laughed at that. "None taken. Unfortunately, our peculiar history set you up for such fascination. It's a lot for such a small community."

"I guess so."

"Give them a little time. You haven't been here long," Carly added.

"Y'all want a nightcap on the front porch?" Leah asked.

"Sounds good," I said.

The guys declined, leaving the three of us to the rocking chairs on the porch.

We drank a glass of wine overlooking the water. I could barely see the bayou in the dark, with only a few ripples reflecting off the moon. Glad for my heavy sweater, I wrapped it more tightly to help with the evening chill. Thankfully, there weren't any bugs this time of year. When I was there last summer, I could hardly step outside without getting bit by giant mosquitos.

I yawned. "I'd better head home now. Thanks for a nice

evening."

"I'm so glad you came tonight, Allison." She reached into her pocket for something. "These are for the gate at the loft." Leah dropped two small keys into my hand.

"Oh, thanks."

I drove home, feeling appreciative for the evening. When I got inside, my phone vibrated, signaling an incoming call. The screen showed that it was from Nick, and I answered. "Hi, Nick."

"Hi, Allison. How are you?"

"Pretty good. I just got home from having dinner at Leah's house with Jake and Carly and Tanner."

"Sounds like fun. I called to tell you that it'll be a few more days at least before I'll be home."

"Oh. Okay. I hope you're okay." Since he didn't seem inclined still to reveal what was going on, there wasn't much else I could say. I'd had enough uncertainty in my life these past couple of years. Now, I found myself doubting Nick.

"Let's talk soon." Questions swirled in my mind about his trip out of town, and it was obvious that he'd made the decision not to share anything besides his location.

THINGS WERE FAR worse down at the Lafayette shop than Nick had first thought. The place was nearly a total loss, with fire, smoke, and water damage to the building and several cars inside the garage and the nearby parking lot. He'd barely slept and spent every waking moment dealing with the situation. Between communications with the fire marshal, the insurance company, and his employees, he was exhausted.

He'd not had a second to contact Allison until earlier this evening. What must she think of him? He'd considered telling her everything, but he simply didn't have the energy to do it. Adding that on top of what he had going on here was too much. It had been nice to hear her voice, but he could tell by her tone that she was expecting some kind of explanation for his absence. He hadn't handled this well at all.

Currently, he was creating an itemized list of everything that had been inside the garage when it caught fire. Everything: tools, tires, cans of oil. All of it. Plus, he had the office equipment and computers to document. All in all, it was a significant loss for the company. They'd been well insured, but every day they were closed was costly for him and the employees.

Thankfully, nobody had been hurt. People were far more important than things, so that was something.

He'd contacted his parents to update them about the fire, and his dad was now a hot mess. Nick hated to heap worry on them, but his dad had only recently retired from the business and was having a hard time letting go of the reins. If he hadn't let them in on the situation, Nick would never hear the end of it. Dad's health scare precipitated his retirement, so Nick was careful how he spoke to his father about the losses. Mom had helped Dad build the business from the ground up and was far tougher now. She knew a lot about how these things worked, so Nick was able to be honest with her.

"I'm sorry you've got to deal with this on your own. I'm not comfortable leaving your father alone, and we sure can't send him down there. He's already pacing the floor. I've checked his blood pressure almost hourly and it's high." Mom was supportive, but this crisis was for Nick to handle.

She did have some suggestions though. "Make sure they put up crime scene tape to deter vandals. Also, get the cameras operating as soon as you can in case this was arson. And if you can manage it, hire a security guard for the next couple of weeks. The hydraulic equipment might be damaged, but it's very expensive, and the bays should be covered with tarps, so they don't get ruined completely." His mother had helped grow the business from the beginning so there was very little about it she didn't know.

Fortunately, he'd done everything she'd suggested besides the security guard. "I'll see about hiring an off-duty or retired officer in the area."

Their years of experience were helpful at a time like this, but Nick had been working for the business long enough to learn mostly what he'd needed to know. He now had to buckle down and give this problem all his attention.

Hopefully, Allison would understand once he explained everything to her. Maybe he would get a minute to let his friends know where he'd disappeared to. And eat a sandwich. And sleep for a few good hours.

He was staying at a local efficiency suites hotel convenient to the auto shop. Nick looked forward to getting through these first crazy few days and then returning to his life as he knew it.

CHAPTER SEVENTEEN

I WOKE UP to the sound of my cell phone ringing.
"Hello?"

"Allison, oh, my goodness. Honey, I wanted to tell you that Mother's had a stroke. She's at Cypress General still in the E.R. They don't have any information besides that yet." Karen sounded distressed.

Nana! Fear gripped me and I tried to control my panic. My heart pounded. It was the same overwhelming sensation I'd had when my mom was taken to the hospital that last time. "Oh, no. I'll get over there as soon as I can." I had to work today, even though it was Saturday, but I was certain Lydia would understand.

"There's no reason for us to all run over just yet. Just keep your phone nearby. When we know more, I'll call."

"I'm so sorry, Karen. I know how scared you must be." I could empathize with her situation a hundred percent, because even though I hadn't known Nana my whole life, she was the one who'd stepped up and taken me in. Nana was the rock of the family. The idea of losing her devastated me. I could only imagine the others' reactions.

"I'm just glad you're here with us, Allison. Having all my girls around me gives me strength. I'll let you know as soon as we have more information."

I was trembling with worry, and it swirled around in my head and into my body. I tried to tamp down the dread. I would go in to work and let Lydia know what was happening, and then take it from there.

A hot shower somewhat restored my frayed nerves. I stopped by the coffee shop near work and grabbed a latte and a scone to boost my energy, and to put something in my stomach. I needed that caffeine and sugar to face the day.

I entered the shop to find Lydia staring at her computer screen in the back office.

She looked up briefly and then refocused. "Oh, hi, Allison. I was going through the inventory spreadsheet and realize we're low on several items. We're barely into November, so I need to do some ordering." Then, she looked at me, a frown forming between her brows. "Is everything okay, dear?"

I pulled off my coat. "Karen called this morning to tell me that Nana had a stroke during the night. I don't know what her condition is yet, but I might need to leave at some point and head for the hospital."

Lydia pulled her glasses off. "Oh no. Of course, you should go. You can leave now if you want."

I shook my head. "Karen said to wait until we know more, so I'll get to work on orders now and try to get ahead in case I leave later."

"Absolutely. Whatever you need. I love your grandmother, as do most of the folks in town. She's been solidly encouraging of all the small businesses here."

"Yes. I've heard her talk about supporting local merchants, and how they're the lifeblood of towns like this."

Lydia sighed. "I wish everybody felt that way."

I sat down at my workbench to begin filling orders. I noticed the first one on top of the stack of invoices was for Tootie Keller. This reminded me that I hadn't answered a text from her about Thanksgiving.

I heard my phone buzz and I immediately dug it from my purse. It was a text from Elizabeth: *I'm sorry to hear about your nana's stroke. Hoping for the best.*

Despite the enmity between the families, I appreciated her kindness.

Thanks, Elizabeth. I haven't heard anything yet on her condition, only that she's in the hospital.

I know Jake is doing everything he can to help. Elizabeth and Jake were co-workers at the hospital, so I assumed they still communicated.

I'm certain he is. Thanks, Elizabeth. We hadn't been in touch since our impromptu lunch a few days ago.

Yes. Talk soon. Texting left a lot to the imagination, so I set my phone down, hoping to get some real news from Karen shortly.

I worked for a couple of hours and decided to inform Nick about Nana's stroke. He would want to know, I was sure, so I texted him and got no immediate response, so I figured whatever he was doing required all his attention. Even though I was beginning to question the nature of Nick's trip, I didn't question his loyalty to my family, especially Nana.

Just before noon, my phone rang. It was Karen's number, so I picked up immediately, heart in my throat. "Hello?"

"Hi Allison. I wanted to give you an update on Momma.

They've done a couple of brain scans, and she's definitely had a stroke. Her speech is a little garbled and her left side is affected. They're still trying to figure out how severe it was." Karen's voice was surprisingly strong, considering she didn't normally do well in a crisis.

"I'm so sorry, Karen. She's been on my mind since you called. Should I come to the hospital?"

"We're all here, so it would be nice to have you with us. Momma's always been the strong one." Karen's voice broke then.

"I'll be right over." I quickly cleaned up my workspace and organized the invoices.

"Was that news about your nana?" Lydia popped her head into the workroom.

"Yes." I filled her in and told her I should go. "I can come in after hours if you need me."

"Don't you worry. I've got a girl I can call to help fill orders if it comes to that. Of course, she's nowhere as good or as fast as you, but she'll do in a pinch."

"Aw, thanks, Lydia. I'll let you know what's happening as soon as I know something."

"Give your family my best, dear."

WHEN I ARRIVED at Cypress General, I inquired about Nana's location at the information desk. The woman manning the desk, Lurline, according to her nametag, reached over and patted my hand. To my credit, I didn't snatch it back. "Oh, honey. I'm so sorry to hear about your nana. Give everybody my love up there, would you? They're all gathered in the third-floor waiting area."

"Okay, thanks."

The hospital brought back memories. And maybe a little fear and panic. Once you've had a near-deadly illness, lost a loved one in a hospital, or spent any time in one, the sights, smells, and sounds imprinted on your psyche.

I stepped out of the elevator and looked around. The center of the floor was set up for waiting families, with several seating vignettes and plenty of indoor green plants. "Allison, over here."

I saw Leah motioning to me. I spotted my two Bertrand sisters, along with Karen, Bob, Tanner, and Jake. "How's she doing?" I asked once I neared the group.

Jake answered, "It's too soon to tell how much damage the stroke caused. She's already showing some improvement in her speech and movement, which is fantastic. But recovery can be tricky given her age."

"I say she'll be running the family from her hospital bed in a day or two." Carly smiled, putting on a brave face for me and the others.

"She does inspire confidence, doesn't she?" I said this out of the firm knowledge that if anyone could recover quickly and completely from this, it would be Nana.

My phone began buzzing due to my ringer being turned on silent. I pulled it from my purse and recognized Nick's number. "Excuse me." I turned and walked several feet from the group.

"Hi, Nick." I pictured his familiar face and realized that I'd missed him.

"Gosh, it's great to hear your voice, Allison. How's Nana?" He sounded exhausted; unlike I'd ever heard him.

I repeated what Jake had said almost verbatim. "They say she's already showing some improvement."

"Gosh, I wish I was there. How's everybody holding up?"

"Karen seems to be doing well, considering. Everybody else has taken a cautiously optimistic 'wait and see' attitude. Nana's such a force in the family that nobody is ready to count her out."

"I'd never bet against Nana." He paused a second. "So, how are you?" His tone was empathetic, and I almost allowed myself the luxury of tearing up and spilling my worries.

I sucked my sadness in and said, "I'm okay for now. Just hoping for the best."

"I'm so sorry I have to be away right now."

"Everything okay?" Once again, I wondered what the heck he was doing.

"Um, not great, but getting there. I'm not sure if anyone told you yet, but one of our auto repair shops has burned nearly to the ground. Nobody was hurt, but it's a huge mess."

"One of your shops?" I was under the impression there was only the one shop in town where he worked as a mechanic. "I'm sorry about the fire."

"Yes. I haven't exactly shared everything about my role in our family business yet. Right now, I have to go because the insurance adjuster just arrived. I'm thinking of you and the family. Please give them all my best."

I was barely keeping up. "Oh. Okay. Take care. I guess

we'll talk soon."

"We will, Allison; I promise." I could hear an unspoken apology and maybe more in his voice.

I was more confused as we hung up than I'd been before. Why had he let me believe he was only a mechanic? I mean, he was a mechanic, but obviously there was more to his life that I'd not yet heard about. He'd intentionally held that information back. I'd had enough uncertainty in my recent past that this really irritated me. I'd shared so much with him in a very short couple of weeks since we'd met.

I was still wondering about our stilted conversation as I made my way back toward the family group. "Everything okay?" Leah asked. "You look confused."

"I guess I am, somewhat. That was Nick on the phone and apparently there was a fire at one of their shops and he's dealing with it. I thought he was a mechanic."

Leah responded, "Oh. Well, he *is* a mechanic—best one in town. But since his daddy had the health scare, he's also the man in charge of ten shops since he's taken over the business last year. I'm surprised you didn't know."

"He led me to believe he worked on cars all day." I didn't want to sound accusing, but I was a little embarrassed to learn something everybody else already knew. Nick and I had spent quite a lot of time talking—mostly about me, I guess, so maybe I didn't show enough interest for him to fill me in on who he really was.

"He usually does, but he also has the business end of things to contend with now," Leah said.

Karen stepped forward then. "Well, *I* can tell you he had a recent girlfriend, who—according to his momma—tried to shame him for *just* being a mechanic, and when she found out how successful he and his family were, she suddenly became much more interested in him. A real gold digger, you know?"

"Hmm. I'm sorry to hear that." I thought about how terrible it would be to be judged or devalued based on a line of work, and my heart went out to Nick. Kind of. I guess I'd thought he trusted me. I'd certainly trusted him and the things he told me. His not sharing more about himself was intentional, which made me uncomfortable.

"It's happened a few times from what I've heard. I'm not trying to gossip you know. Just fill in the blanks for you. So, he doesn't automatically trust new women he meets."

Nick and I had only gone out a few times, but we'd developed a kind of closeness, and I knew it wasn't just on my part, so being led to believe something that wasn't exactly accurate felt like a lie to me. I'd been so keen recently on finding truth in other parts of my life that it rankled. Nick wasn't the only one with trust issues. I'd been walloped by the doubting bug since the day I'd found out I was adopted. So, yes, I got it, but I'd been so open with Nick—unusually so.

I did my best to shake off the funk my conversation with Nick stirred up. "So, what's the next step?" I asked Jake.

"They'll continue to monitor her vitals, neurological and motor functions, and do blood work and decide how at risk she might be for this to happen again. Right now, she's in great hands, so unfortunately all we can do as her family is wait on progress reports. Since she's in the ICU, only two visitors are allowed every four hours."

"Leah and I went in to see her before anyone else arrived, so you girls can go in next if you want." Karen indicated me and Carly since we were standing next to each other.

"When are visiting hours?" I asked.

Jake checked his watch. "In about ten minutes."

CHAPTER EIGHTEEN

BEEPING MACHINES WITH tiny lights of all colors filled Nana's room, and I immediately responded with an elevated heart rate and heavy breathing. The near-panic I'd felt both during my mom's stay in the hospital and for mine returned. "Are you okay?" Carly asked with a frown of concern as she looked at me. "Your face is pale."

"I'll be okay. Hospitals do this to me."

"I'm not surprised after what you went through." She grabbed my hand as we approached the bed. Nana, who'd always seemed stronger and healthier than all of us lay there with her eyes closed, appearing older than I'd ever seen her. She opened her eyes suddenly, surprising us both. "Y'all gonna help me get outta this bed?" Her speech sounded like she had marbles rolling around in her mouth and her left cheek drooped just a little.

"Hey, Nana," Carly spoke first. "We came to see how they were treating you in here."

Nana turned her head slightly to get a better look at us. "I want to go home."

I took her right hand. "We want you to come home just as soon as the doctors say it's okay. You know how they are with their tests."

Nana frowned, then squeezed my hand. "Happy to see

you girls."

"Us too," I said.

"Nana, we're all here for you, so let us know if you need anything while you're in here," Carly said.

"Nana, you get some rest now." I hoped she hadn't felt my hand trembling or picked up on my fear for her.

"Love you girls." She waved at us with her right hand.

"Love you," we chimed together.

After we'd gotten out of the room and into the hallway, I let out the breath I'd been holding. "She looks pretty good, considering."

Carly nodded. "Yeah, but it freaks me out seeing her like that and not on her feet. She's always the one in charge. I have a feeling she won't take this lying down." Then we both laughed a little. "Well, you know what I mean." One of the things I liked most about my Bertrand sisters was how they kept a sense of humor in the face of adversity. No matter how serious things became, they could still laugh.

"I'm guessing we can expect a visit from Father Felix and his two remaining nuns, Sisters Gladys and Helen anytime now. Momma might get her wish to introduce the two of you after all."

I snorted at that because I'd heard all about the two octogenarian nuns from Karen. "I guess a few prayers wouldn't hurt though." In the current situation, prayers were all we had since nothing about Nana's stroke was under anyone's control. "I probably should go back to work for a few more hours so I don't get behind on orders."

"If you want to scoot out from here and avoid the padre and his posse, I'll tell them you had to go back to work and will check in later."

I nodded. "But please keep me posted. I can come back at a moment's notice."

NICK WAS FINALLY able to see his way clear to handle things at the shop by phone and by FaceTime. Once the insurance adjuster had gone over everything with a fine-tooth comb, Nick felt much better about leaving. Suzie, the store manager, was a whiz, so instead of managing the office over the next few weeks, she would take calls and set up appointments for the contractor and his subs to come out and have a look. Nick would agree on a reconstruction schedule and come back when he was needed. Fortunately, the hydraulic car lifts were underground and had missed the worst of the fire, so most of the work would be focused on rebuilding the actual structure and replacing stock and tools.

Almost the second Nick got in his SUV, he dialed Allison's number. Her reaction earlier when he told her he'd not been totally honest with her had him worried a little. That, and he was concerned about Nana.

She answered on the second ring. "Hello?"

"Hey there. I just left Lafayette and now I'm headed home and wanted to check on Nana, and on you."

"Oh, hey, Nick. How are things with the shop?"

"Getting there. It took several days to go through the process with the adjuster and the contractor. We were fortunate to find someone available to start the rebuild immediately."

"I'm glad to hear it. I just left the hospital after seeing Nana for the first time. She's stable and improving, but she's not happy about being there confined to a bed, I'll tell you that."

Nick had known Nana Elise his entire life, and he knew her to be a kind but stubborn woman. "No, I guess not, but I'm glad to hear she's coming along. So, how are things with you?" Nick held his breath waiting for her reply.

"Things are okay so far. I'm headed now to get a phone at Walmart."

"I'm so sorry I couldn't take you to Shreveport to get one. But you're in a pinch, and Walmart has a decent selection."

"No problem. You had to deal with an emergency." But there were words she hadn't said yet. She'd cooled off since their earlier conversation. She was cordial, but something was missing.

Nick paused, not quite sure how to approach the subject. "So, I'm not sure what you've heard, but I wanted to come clean about everything with you. I'm sorry for not telling you before I left town."

"Listen, we're both under stress right now so we can talk when you get back?" she asked.

It would be selfish to expect that she hear him out over the phone while she dashed around town running errands. Instead, he asked, "Do you have plans this evening?"

She hesitated. "I've got to go back to work as soon as I get my phone taken care of, but if you want to come by later after work, I guess that would be okay. How about seven?"

He breathed a sigh of relief that she'd agreed to see him,

but she still sounded...distant. "I've missed you, Allison." He pictured her face as he said it.

"I've missed you too, Nick. But I admit that I'm confused about things right now."

He suddenly felt the exhaustion settle in his bones, so he said, "I'll meet you at your house this evening."

"See you then."

I DIDN'T HAVE time to stop and talk to Nick, so I put him off. This would be an important conversation, so it was worth waiting until there were fewer distractions.

I hadn't eaten anything yet but skipping lunch wouldn't kill me, and I wanted to get back to the shop as soon as possible. I couldn't let Lydia down during her busiest season.

As I entered Walmart, "Jingle Bells" was playing on the store's speakers. There were Christmas displays everywhere, touting lower prices and great deals. I mostly ignored the curious looks I received from shoppers as they recognized me. I mean, I didn't look funny, did I? The man at the electronics counter greeted me with a smile, his Santa hat slightly askew. "What can I get for you today?"

"I need a new phone." I held up my aging device.

We discussed features and he showed me several options. I pointed at one through the glass and he pulled out the small box. "You'd do better if you just transferred the service from one to the other."

On it went until I finally insisted that I was in a hurry and needed to get going.

"Well, hello there. Allison, is it?" A woman about Karen's age with drawn-on eyebrows pulled up with her shopping cart beside mine. "I'm Cynthia Breedlove, Judge Breedlove's wife. My husband and your daddy have worked together for years as district judges, and your momma and I are both members at the garden club in town. How's Arthur holding up? And Elise? I heard she's had a stroke, poor dear."

I tried to smile at the woman; I did. But I was picking up on insincerity in every word. "It's nice to meet you, Mrs. Breedlove—"

"Call me Cynthia. Please," she interrupted.

"Cynthia. The judge is fine, and so is Nana. Thanks for asking."

"Oh, but I heard—"

I decided the woman needed no further ammunition from my lips. "Excuse me, I've got to finish up here." I turned my back to her, putting an end to this gossip quest.

"How rude." She huffed from behind me, and as she hurriedly stalked off, I could hear the squeak of a bad wheel on her cart all the way through the store.

"You don't want to make an enemy of that one," the clerk muttered. "Might find a parking ticket on your car by the time you get out of here, if you know what I mean."

I rolled my eyes and handed him my credit card. The strangeness around here seemed unending. I was looking forward to seeing Nick this evening. He'd been my person since I'd arrived. My voice of reason and the one who helped me laugh about it all. Right now, I was struggling to find the humor.

I grabbed a bag of my favorite chocolates on the way to

the front of the store. As I checked out, the cashier smiled timidly at me. "I hope your nana is okay. I heard she had a stroke. Everybody loves Ms. Elise here in town, and we're praying for her." Nana somehow managed to spread good feelings wherever she went, and I guess I should take a page from that book, so I wasn't compared to Karen or Elizabeth instead.

"She's faring well right now. Thanks for asking and for the prayers." The girl, Heidi, according to her nametag, had a sweet face and a kind manner. So different from the harridan who'd squeaked her way through the store a few minutes ago.

"Thanks again, Heidi. I'll let her know."

There was no parking ticket on my car when I got outside to the lot. That was good news, at least.

I quickly group-texted my new, local number to my immediate family. I could go through later and figure out who else I'd want to share it with. I kept the old phone, so I had all the contacts, which were sadly few aside from my old clients. The clerk assured me that Verizon would be a better carrier for me in Cypress Bayou.

BY THE TIME I'd finished the day's orders at Donovan's, it was past dark, and as I prepared to depart for home, my anticipation at seeing Nick after work filled me with relief. Relief that he was back home safely and that I would see him soon. Lydia had given me a key to the shop just before she'd left for the day. So, I locked up and set the store's alarm and then texted Nick.

Hi Nick, I'm about to leave Donovan's, so I'll be home in a couple minutes.

He answered immediately. *I'll be right over.*

I breathed an instant sigh of relief. I wanted to clear the air with Nick, but I also needed him to understand how important the whole truth was to me. I never wanted to find out secrets from other people as long as we were—whatever we were.

Nick was there within five minutes. I saw him as he approached the front door and noticed the stubble on his jaw. It was a good look on him. I suppressed a strong urge to throw my arms around his neck the second I opened the door for him.

Nick, on the other hand, did not withhold the urge to hug me tight. "I've missed you." I melted into his embrace like it was home, inhaling his scent, and not wanting it to end.

When we drew apart, our eyes connected, and I could see the question in his golden-brown eyes. The urge to kiss him was unbelievably strong, but I tore my gaze away and moved toward the kitchen. "Beer?" I offered and he nodded and took a seat at the kitchen island.

Nick's presence comforted me. I knew in my heart that Nana was doing well, but her illness and the feeling that things weren't right between Nick and me were causing me stress unlike I'd had since coming here. "I'm glad you came over. Sorry I was distracted earlier."

"No problem. I had to give my parents a full accounting of my trip, so I managed to get that over with." He got quiet for a few seconds and said, "Allison, I couldn't sleep for worrying about your opinion of me. I admit that I intentionally held off telling you about my family business because things were so easy between us, and you liked me for the simple mechanic you thought me to be."

"What's wrong with being a mechanic?" I asked, not understanding why that was such a big deal.

"I've been hurt before, and I guess I didn't want to take a chance of seeing something change in your eyes when you learned the truth. That sounds silly and opposite of what I'd normally think. It's not that I believed you'd be more interested in me because of my career, I just wanted things to stay as they were."

I nodded. "Getting to know you is the best thing that's happened since I moved to Cypress Bayou. That's why I was so upset when I found out you weren't being completely honest with me. I've got a problem with trust—same as you, it seems."

I stood across the bar, and he reached out for my hands. "I promise I'll never keep anything from you going forward. You've shared yourself with me and I'll do the same."

"Thanks, Nick. That means so much." *But where are we headed? Do I want to make promises?* The thought hit me as soon as I uttered the words that sounded so promising to him and to me.

My new phone rang then, and normally I wouldn't have answered at such a sweet moment. "Sorry. It might be about Nana."

He nodded. "Of course you should answer."

CHAPTER NINETEEN

"Nana's had another stroke." Leah's words had me drowning in worry. "We're gathering at the hospital to wait on the doctor's report. Momma's not handling it well, so she needs our support."

"O-Okay. I'll be right over." My mind was a hive of bad outcomes. I'd realized years ago that my nature was the glass half empty, and when things happened beyond my control, I tended to head back there.

"What is it?" Nick asked. "What's happened?"

I took a deep breath to try and steady my emotions. "It's Nana. She's had another stroke."

"I'll drive you to the hospital."

"Thanks, Nick."

I clutched my purse and said almost nothing on the way to Cypress General, the fear almost overwhelming me.

"You okay?" Nick asked gently.

I shook my head, but I didn't look at him—I couldn't. My emotions were threatening to burst, and it wouldn't take much to blow the top off of them.

"Here we go." He put the truck in park and met me at the passenger's side door. He didn't ask any more questions until we got inside. "Third floor?"

I nodded.

We rode the elevator to the same waiting area where we'd all met after Nana's first stroke, and just as before, the family was gathered, quietly chatting when we arrived. "Any news?" I asked as soon as they were in earshot.

"Nothing yet," Jake answered, looking grim. "We're waiting on more tests."

Nick greeted everyone quietly, communicating his best wishes.

I noticed Karen sitting silently on the low sofa, her face streaked with tears. I sat down next to her and took her hand. "Nana's a strong woman."

Karen turned and faced me then. "When you were born, she told me I didn't have to give you up and that we would figure things out together. But I was too scared to learn what that life might be. Please don't blame her for my sins."

Her words hit me in the heart, and it took me a few seconds to formulate an appropriate response. "I've forgiven you, Karen. It's time you forgave yourself."

"I just wanted you to know that she wanted to keep you with us. I needed you to understand that she was blameless. In case—you know." Fresh tears dripped from her lashes, which caused me to tear up as well.

I placed my arm around her shoulders. "I don't blame either of you anymore." I was pretty sure that was true, and it was what Karen needed to hear right now. There was no changing the past and it was up to me to deal with it.

An older man in blue scrubs approached and we both stood. "Elise is on a ventilator to regulate her breathing. We're hoping she will stabilize soon."

A ventilator. The word caused me such anxiety. They'd

put Mom on a ventilator the day before she'd died.

Jake asked, "Is there any other treatment for now?"

"She's on blood thinners and her heart is in A-fib, but once her breathing regulates, we should be able to take her off the ventilator and work toward regulating her heart rhythm."

"When will we know if she's improving?" Carly asked. She stood holding hands with Tanner.

"A day or two should give us some indication."

Jake thanked the surgeon.

There had to be something to do in the meantime, so I offered, "Should I go and stay at Nana's house and feed Beaux? Water her plants, maybe?"

"Nana is a steadfast plant-waterer, and Beaux likely feels like he's been deserted, so that's a nice idea if it doesn't inconvenience you, Allison," Leah said. "We've been taking turns feeding Beaux so far."

I nodded. "Okay. I'll head over there tonight." I couldn't do nothing. At least this way I would feel like I was helping Nana in some way.

I felt Nick beside me, silently comforting me. "I'll follow you there later and make sure everything's okay at the house."

I looked up at him. "Thank you." Though I was certain that everything at Nana's house was in order, I appreciated his wanting to help.

"We can take shifts at the hospital."

"What about Thanksgiving dinner?" Karen asked. Thanksgiving was the day after tomorrow. "We've never had Thanksgiving without Momma."

Everyone nodded. "I could do it at my house," Leah suggested.

"I can't help but think Momma would want to stick with tradition and have the meal at her house, even without her there," Karen said. "We can all bring the food in."

"I'll do the turkey if you all want to bring the sides," I offered.

"I thought you didn't cook." Jake raised his brows in question at me.

"I don't cook much, but I learned how to brine and roast a turkey with stuffing when my mom was sick and unable to do it."

"I hate to think about Thanksgiving without Nana," Carly said, shaking her head. "But I'm willing if y'all are. I'll bring the sweet potato casserole and a salad." And so it went. They covered all the main dishes and planned to meet up at Nana's house Thursday at noon.

"Let me know which dishes to use and I'll set the table." I'd tried so hard to make things special for Mom when she could no longer get around, so I'd searched a lot of YouTube videos to learn how it was done. Since I was crafty, I'd tried my best to make every holiday special during that last year of her life.

"I'll come by and find what we need for the table," Karen said. "You know Momma likes things a certain way." Everyone nodded at that statement. Nana was nothing if not specific and thorough when it came to entertaining.

I think planning—for anything at this point—was more helpful than standing around with our hands in our pockets wondering what we should do. Thanksgiving dinner together gave us all something to focus on, so our minds didn't go to the bad places.

We stayed together, talking quietly for a few hours for Karen's benefit. But the hospital heebie-jeebies were a real thing with me, so I finally said, "I'm going to head over to my place for some clothes and then to Nana's to check on Beaux."

"Oh, here. I've got a key to Nana's house." Karen picked up her purse from the table beside the sofa.

"I've still got one from when I stayed with her before. She insisted I keep it." I clearly remembered when I'd tried to return the key just before I'd gone back to Illinois.

"Okay. Let us know if you need anything to get ready for Thursday," Leah said and then turned to Nick. "Thanks for coming. I know Nana would appreciate your support."

Nobody seemed to think his coming with me to such a close family crisis gathering was odd. It helped me understand the bond he shared with my family. But it also concerned me that if things didn't work out for us as a couple, that bond might be damaged. I hated thinking about the what-ifs, but my whole life was a big *what-if* right now.

I realized I was doing it again—that glass-half-empty thing I did, so I forced my thoughts in a different direction. I would enjoy the time spent with Nick and not worry about any possible future regrets at the moment. "Are you ready?" I asked.

"Yes. I'll head out and pull up the truck while you finish." I assumed this was his way of making himself scarce in case I wanted a minute alone with family.

"Thanks, Nick."

As I drove through the darkened streets, I noticed the many homes and businesses strung with colorful lights. It reminded me of how close we were to the holidays. Of course, people around here didn't wait until after Thanksgiving to decorate for Christmas. As an interior designer, that didn't bother me. Christmas was a decorating holiday. Thanksgiving, not so much.

Nick insisted on following me to Nana's after I'd gone by my apartment and packed up several days' worth of clothes and personal items.

Nana's house was unusually dark when we arrived save the one lamp in the living room. Beaux looked up from the wingback chair beside the lamp when we entered the sitting area. "Hey, buddy." I had a rush of sympathy for the old guy who'd seen so much life. I imagined he was lonely without Nana's constant company. I stroked his multi-colored fur down his back and behind his ears and was rewarded by hearing him purr and knead his paws against the chair's fabric.

"You think Nana's got something to eat in here? I'm starving." Nick was beside me.

I'd been hungry all afternoon after skipping lunch. "Me too. I can't imagine that she doesn't. Her refrigerator is usually packed with food." I flipped on the kitchen light and checked out what our options were. "Looks like leftover chicken enchiladas in the freezer and a container of chili. Sound good?" I turned to Nick and held up both containers. Nana always marked the leftovers as to what they were and when they were prepared.

"Sounds fantastic." We worked together heating up the food and dishing it out on two plates.

I found some corn chips in the pantry, and salsa in the fridge to add to our unexpected dinner. "It smells awesome." I inhaled the spicy aroma and my stomach growled.

"Nana's never made anything that wasn't awesome that I know of." We pulled up stools and ate at the bar. It seemed intimate, the two of us sitting together in Nana's kitchen.

We tidied up from our dinner and kind of looked at each other. "Well, I guess we could watch some TV," I suggested, knowing there wasn't much else to do besides board games.

We moved to the parlor in the front room, which had a small but comfortable sofa and a TV.

"Any ideas on shows or movies?" he asked.

I laughed at his taking charge of the remote. "You're such a guy."

"What do you mean by that?"

"The way you grabbed that remote without hesitation." I was still smiling, but I'd thrown him off guard.

"So, do you want the remote?" He offered it to me. "I'm perfectly happy for you to be in charge."

"No, it was just an observation."

"Well, I can tell you that I know every channel by heart, from before I got my smart TV. Can you say the same?" Nick challenged me.

"Nope. I can't." So that was obviously settled. Here we were bickering like old married people over who controlled the remote control. It was fun, and despite the situation we faced, we were together, and that felt right to me in the moment.

"Did you ever watch *Lost* back when it was on?"

"No, I never got into it, but I'm willing to give it a try."

"Looks like a full, first-season marathon starting in a few minutes." He used the channel guide to enter the station. "I'm assuming Nana doesn't have any smart TVs?"

"Don't assume. There are two upstairs. One in her bedroom so she can watch her programs and the other in the spare bedroom where I stayed after I got out of the hospital. She bought it so I would have plenty to keep me entertained during my recovery, since it took several weeks for me to get back on my feet." But I didn't suggest we go in the bedroom for obvious reasons. This room was just fine.

"I heard a little about your recovery from my mom. She and Karen sometimes meet for lunch or bingo. But it doesn't surprise me at all that Nana bought you a TV."

I ignored the part where he said he'd gotten the scoop from his mom via Karen. "Yes, Nana was wonderful to me during my recovery."

"Well, we can do this for now unless the commercials start to drive us crazy."

The music for *Lost* came on then, signaling the start of the show.

NICK WOKE UP with a cramp in his neck and Allison's head against his shoulder. He could smell her shampoo with its hints of lemon and had a sudden urge to put his arm around her like he'd done earlier. But he couldn't turn this into a romantic situation with Nana's condition.

Instead, he gently eased into a lying position with her head against the velvet sofa pillow.

She woke just as he'd gotten her in a better position. "Oh, hey. Sorry I conked out on you." She yawned and stretched.

"You've had a busy day—we both have."

The glow of the screen filled the darkened room, and Allison sat up to rub the stiffness in her neck and shoulders.

"May I?" Nick moved his hands to both sides of her neck and began kneading the muscles between her shoulder blades.

She moaned slightly. The pressure from his thumbs must have hit all the right places. "Thank you for everything, Nick. What would I do without you?"

She appeared a little embarrassed to have said those words aloud, so Nick said, "I'm not planning on going anywhere."

She leaned back into his arms then. He was content to have her this close.

"Do you want me to stay here with you tonight? I mean, not with you, but in the house?" He hoped she didn't take that wrong.

"I'll be fine, so you should go home and get some sleep." She gave him a tired smile as she turned a little to face him. He could see the fatigue etched on her face.

He nodded, taking his cue from her. His staying at Nana's house with her alone tonight could mean more gossip for her, and gossip could come from anywhere. Nick was willing to weather it if Allison needed him, but the exhaustion had settled in from his trip and he was due a good night's sleep in his own bed.

"Well, I'll head out now if you're okay." He paid close attention to her response in case she was putting on a brave face for his benefit.

"I'm okay, Nick. I've lived alone for the past two years, and it doesn't bother me to be here by myself."

"Let me hear from you in the morning when you get any news on Nana." He was having a hard time leaving her alone, despite her words.

"I'll likely sleep like the dead tonight, so don't worry about me." Sleep was definitely what she needed. The stress and worry during all of this had taken its toll.

Nick wanted to put his arms around her, to reassure her, but he hesitated going farther down that path when they were both ragged with exhaustion.

CHAPTER TWENTY

I WOKE EARLY, and despite my fitful night, I dragged myself out of bed and to the kitchen, where I planned to make a large pot of coffee. My cell rang just as I pressed the start button on the coffee maker.

It was Leah. "Good morning. I wanted to give you an update on Nana's condition. She's off the ventilator and wide awake now. Her heart's still in A-Fib but the doctors think that it will go back into a normal rhythm now that her breathing is regular again. If it doesn't soon, they plan to try and shock it back."

I sighed in relief. "That all sounds promising. Thanks for calling."

"How are you doing at Nana's? Is Beaux okay?" Leah asked.

"I'm doing pretty well besides a sleepless night. I'm going after work to get the turkey at the grocery store."

"How long do you think you'll stay at Nana's house?" Leah asked.

"I'll be happy to stay here until she comes home so I can help her get back on her feet. I don't have any reason not to."

I heard Leah's relieved sigh. "Thanks so much. I'm headed to New Orleans today to kick off a gallery show in

Bywater. I'll be back tomorrow early, but Momma gets stressy, you know, so I'm relieved to know you're there, and between you and Carly, y'all can handle her. It usually takes Nana, me, and Carly to deal with her in a crisis." Leah owned an art gallery in New Orleans and often went there to check in on her managers and help plan events.

"I'm working today, but after that, I'll be here brining a turkey and making stuffing."

"Great. I'll coordinate with Momma and let her know the plan. I hate leaving town in the middle of all of this, but I've got commitments down South."

"Drive safely today." I said it automatically, but I realized how much I wanted and needed my new people to be safe. I felt the slight shift in the sand, and it surprised me.

"Thanks, Allison."

Helping to coordinate logistics within the family made me feel like I was an important part of things. With the years of togetherness they'd all had, I was inching toward believing I could someday be one of them. And since I'd cared for my mom for so long, it felt natural to step up and do the same for Nana.

Besides Karen's obvious weirdness and inappropriate outbursts, the others had done their best to welcome me and worked to help me acclimate. The biggest issue was clearly me and my attitude, or maybe it was a huge dose of insecurity—or both. I'd come a long way from the angry tween and teen who'd struggled with the feelings of abandonment after my mom broke the news of my adoption. Meeting the Bertrands had been the best medicine for my soul, even though I still carried around some obviously deep-seated angst over it.

I pulled myself out of the gunky thoughts and decided to take the small win.

As I drove to work, I passed a truck that looked a bit like Nick's, which brought him immediately to mind. Last night, I was so impacted with Nana's health drama that I'd pretty much dismissed Nick in favor of sleep, though I could see that he was in need of some sleep as well.

I had no business starting a new relationship while I tried to figure myself out. But I'd decided to give myself a little grace at the moment. Baby steps were best with regards to my life right now.

As I drove through downtown, I noticed that in the last day, the entire downtown had completed its transformation to a Christmas wonderland. Every streetlamp pole was wrapped with sparkling red garland topped by the boughs we'd made for them, and every storefront was outfitted in full holiday splendor. From snowmen to Christmas trees, and the many gorgeous wreaths hung on every front door.

But when I passed my apartment and headed to Donovan Interiors, I also noticed that the defunct soap store stuck out like a sore thumb, as did my ungarnished balcony. I would need to remedy that as soon as possible. But when? Maybe I could make a plan during lunch. My workday would be short, because I needed to get home to Nana's to do Thanksgiving prep.

Lydia was already at the shop, and I found her surrounded by boxes in the workroom. She turned at hearing me enter. "Allison dear, are you okay? How's Elise today?"

I told Lydia about Nana's second stroke.

"Oh dear. I hate to hear it."

It wouldn't have surprised me if she didn't already know, the way information traveled in this town. I guess I was getting used to people knowing my business. And I believed that Lydia was truly concerned for my welfare and for Nana's. "It was a little scary, but things appear to be moving in the right direction now."

"Listen, I understand if you aren't up for working today." Her tone implied empathy for my situation.

"Thanks, Lydia. I think working is the best thing I can do now. Plus, I know we've got tons to do around here."

"I certainly can use the help, that's for sure. The supplies came in just in time to get these orders done by their promised delivery dates."

I rolled up the sleeves to my loose-fitting red and black flannel button-up. I'd hoped that dressing in festive holiday colors might help improve my mood. Lydia and I quickly checked the boxes against the packing slips and organized the supplies. Some went to the closet in the storeroom and others to our workspaces. Afterward, we began working on the newest client orders together.

I shared with Lydia that I planned to stay at Nana's house with Beaux for now and our plan for Thanksgiving without Nana present.

"How kind. Sounds like you've got some prep to do after work?" Lydia asked.

"I'd hoped to leave as close to five as possible. Karen is going to help out with the table décor."

"That shouldn't be a problem. We'll get everything we can done by then, and if we don't, we can finish tomorrow."

"Thanks for being so considerate, Lydia. I can bring some of this to her house with me and work on it at home if you don't mind. I could set up in the den and work on orders."

"That's a great plan. It doesn't matter to me if you're here or there. I've no doubt that you'll be as efficient as always."

"That would be awesome. My car is big enough to carry plenty of supplies and completed orders. I'm happy to deliver the ones who need it."

"Great idea. I've got a list of clients I deliver to, and you can work on their orders at home. When you're finished with them, you can do the delivery. Just let me know when you want to come in to get more supplies. I mean, there's no real reason for you to be here if you can do it from home. And you'll promise to let me know if you work overtime?"

"Wow, thanks. That will take some of the pressure off Karen and my sisters, for sure."

We continued working for a little while in silence. As I wired in small angel into the wreath I was working on, I looked up and caught Lydia watching me.

"So, I was thinking some more about your opening a shop here in town. I think there's room for it."

Her words surprised me. I honestly hadn't given it another thought. "Hmm. I haven't decided if I'm going to stay here long term, but if I do, it might be a valid idea."

"Just think about it, Allison. There's no sense in working for somebody else when you could be your own boss and business owner. You could have a workroom and sell florals, candles, soaps, and gifts. I do mostly interior design, so you could make the things, I could buy them from you, and we would both have our own lane. Plus, you could sell to the public and wholesale. We're down a soap store around here, you know?"

The idea of having my own business thrilled me. It always had, but the timing hadn't ever been right. "I'll think about it some more." I twisted a turtle dove into the centerpiece I was now working on. "Oh, I wanted to ask if you had any spare garland I could use to decorate my balcony and the storefront downstairs. They both look so sad and out of place with all the festive Christmas décor on Front Street. I'll be happy to buy it from you." I'd noticed a surplus of holiday greenery in the back of the storeroom.

"Nonsense. I've got lots of stuff back there. Most of it has been used before, so have a look and take what you need. I tend to recycle things year to year, so I hang on to the spares." She waved a hand in the direction of the storeroom.

"I'll have a look at lunchtime. Thanks." We worked in near-silence until almost noon, both focusing on getting the orders filled as quickly as possible.

I got a text from Nick just before noon. *Can you meet me for lunch?*

I answered: *I've got something I need to do during my lunch hour here in the shop.*

Him: *Okay. Can I bring something by for you?*

Sounds good. I'm flexible about the food, so you choose, and then you can help me with something while you're here.

Nick answered: *Happy to help in any way. Picking up po' boys.*

I sent him a thumbs-up emoji. "Lydia, Nick is bringing lunch by for me, and we're going to dig through the stored garland in back, so I'll be there if you need me."

Lydia grinned in a knowing way. "Well, don't worry, I won't disturb the two of you."

I didn't even try to explain that we were just friends.

NICK STOPPED AT the café a few spaces down from Donovan Interiors to pick up the po' boys for them. He was thrilled that Allison agreed to lunch with everything she had going on right now. He frankly wanted to lay eyes on her to make sure she was okay.

"Hey, Nick, I heard about Miss Elise's second stroke. Give Allison my best." His buddy Jack stood nearby waiting for an order.

"I'm meeting her for lunch. I'll pass along your thoughts." Nick avoided giving a full explanation of Nana's condition because the lunch crowd was listening. A quick glance around told him that most everyone inside the diner was either a friendly acquaintance or somebody he recognized, and Nick well understood that most would repeat anything they heard him say, possibly inaccurately, to their co-workers in businesses around town.

The last thing Nick wanted was to feed gossip firsthand to the locals—the very thing about being here in Cypress Bayou that Allison detested. His goal was for her to make it her permanent home, and everything he did and said moving forward must be to that end. No more missteps when it came to Allison. She needed his support and honesty, and nothing less.

Nick retrieved his order from the counter and stepped outside into the cold November sunshine. The colorful holiday vibe was all over town now and he couldn't wait for Allison to experience her first Christmas Festival.

When Nick arrived at the interiors shop, he didn't see anyone. "Hello? Allison?" he called before sticking his head through the doorway of the office in back.

Lydia was eating a sandwich and staring at the screen of her computer. "Oh, hey, Nick. Allison is digging for some things in the storeroom. Go on back. She's expecting you." She pointed behind her toward a door.

"Thanks, Lydia."

When Nick entered, he saw a large, moving blob of greenery coming toward him. Allison was underneath. "Oh, hey. Let me help with this." He lifted her burden and placed it to the side of the door. "This okay?"

"Yes, thanks. Something smells good." She dusted off her hands and wiped them on her jeans. "I guess I'd better go wash up. I'll be just a minute. We can go into the breakroom by Lydia's office to eat."

By the time Allison got back, he'd pulled the to-go containers from the paper bag and placed them both on the table. "I hope you like shrimp and french fries."

"My mouth is watering just thinking about it." She bit into the fried shrimp po' boy with gusto. "Mmm. So good."

"It's my favorite place to get an oyster po' boy in town." They ate in silence for a few minutes before Nick approached his reason for coming.

"I wanted to check in with you and see how you're feeling today. It occurred to me last night that all this stress and sleeplessness isn't good for you because you're still recovering."

She stopped eating and their eyes met. "I know. But once Nana is out of the woods completely I think it won't be so stressful." She took a sip of her drink and continued the eye contact. "I appreciate your considering my health in all of this. I tend to put one foot in front and repeat without thinking about it."

"And here I bring you a heart attack sandwich." He pointed to the nearly eaten po' boy.

She laughed at his description of her po' boy. "You brought me exactly what I needed to help get me through all of this. And you dropped everything and brought me to the hospital last night."

"I was glad to be there with you."

She nodded. "I'm just saying that I recognize that it was a sacrifice."

"I mean, I'm a nice guy, but you're not just anybody to me." Nick needed to make it clear to her that he was all in and to prove it.

There was a brief silence as Allison appeared to consider that. "Everything is in a state of uncertainty in my life, and I don't want to lead you on, as much as I like you." She wrinkled her brow. "I don't know what the best plan for my future is yet."

Nick was determined not to let her slip away from him. He was certain her place was here in Cypress Bayou with her family—and hopefully with him. "Well, I more than like you already, and I'm willing to take that chance if you'll let me. Allow me to be your friend with benefits, and by benefits I mean a friend who will go out on a limb for you or with you. I want you to call on me if you need something—anything. Don't let your doubt or fear keep you from feeling whatever it is you might feel."

She looked him directly in the eye then, her expression dead serious. "I realize this is as much a risk for you as it is for me, and I appreciate how much you've put yourself out there for me already.

He answered just as directly. "I'm willing to risk it all, Allison. I know that you're treading lightly, so I'll stop there. Now, how can I help with all of this?" He pointed to the excessive amounts of Christmas greenery.

She smiled then, probably appreciating his change of subject as much as the offer of his help. "I need to decorate my apartment's balcony, and I want to do something to liven up the space downstairs. Just because the store closed doesn't mean it has to look so dismal and unfestive."

"Okay, tell me what to carry and I'll put it in your car."

They got to work loading the garland and a tub filled with other decorations from the storeroom shelves into Allison's SUV. He assumed she had a vision about how to use all the stuff.

"Can I meet you here Saturday morning and help you put this up?" Tomorrow was Thanksgiving, so it would have to wait until after.

"It's too much to ask, Nick. I won't use you for manual labor—or more manual labor." She noticed the load in his arms as she said it.

"I'm offering, and keep in mind our conversation from about three minutes ago. I want to know you better and the only way to do that is to spend time together, even if it's doing manual labor with you or for you."

"Then I guess I'll see you Saturday morning."

CHAPTER TWENTY-ONE

I LEFT WORK and headed straight to the grocery, along with every other individual in town who didn't get their Thanksgiving goods ahead of time. I smiled and nodded in response to people greeting me while I worked my way through the store—which was surprisingly well stocked for it being so close to the big day.

I'd made a comprehensive list of all the things I might need. Honestly, I had no idea how much the others would bring to Nana's, so I got ice, soft drinks, and a yummy-looking pumpkin pie with a pecan streusel topping. Plus, the turkey and salt for brine, for which I sighed in relief when I go to the meat department and noticed there were still several big ones left. I'd never waited this long to buy the turkey because the stores tended to run out close to Thanksgiving Day. And I'd never bought such an enormous bird.

I was contemplating a brining bag when I remembered that Beaux needed food. I completed my shopping and stood in one of the long ant-trail lines that curved sideways to allow shoppers to pass. I noticed a text from Carly that said Nana was still stable and that her heart rhythm was improving. I breathed a thankful sigh of relief at that bit of good news.

Karen was due to arrive at Nana's house anytime to help

with prep and to set the table with the *right* dishes and glassware; in fact, she might already be there. My birth mother was a stickler for details when it came to holidays and celebrations. Her vow renewal with Bob had been an incredible show of planning and details. I imagined Thanksgiving would be no less intentional.

I quickly responded: *I'm so relieved, Carly.*

As I waited for my card to process, I heard a woman's voice over the din of beeping scanners. "Allison!"

I instinctively turned toward the front of the store from where I'd heard the woman call my name. It was Tootie Keller about thirty feet away, and she was waving at me, her hand a blur of bright red nails mixed with the sparkle of the huge diamond that graced her hand.

I waved and put a smile on. I wasn't about to yell back across the store and create a spectacle, though Tootie didn't seem to mind one. They'd invited me to Thanksgiving dinner at the Keller home, but I'd had to decline because Thanksgiving with the Bertrands wasn't even a question. I'd promised the Kellers that I'd swing by over the weekend.

Thankfully, Tootie turned and headed outside with her shopping cart. I'd resisted the urge to duck my head or to roll my eyes at her. People were staring now that she'd drawn their attention to me. I'm sure they were staring at her as well since she was the wife of the judge.

I finally made it outside and shivered a little, as the temps seemed to be dropping. It had been a gorgeous November day, and the evening sunset was especially colorful, with its layers of oranges, yellows, and reds.

I headed to Nana's in my loaded-down car. In addition

A BAYOU CHRISTMAS

to groceries, Nick and I had shoved an obscene amount of stuff to bedeck the outside of my apartment and the façade below on Saturday.

I wanted to get all the prep for Thanksgiving done tonight so I would have time in the morning to cook without stress. As I was unloading the car, I got a call from Lisa—Tanner and Jake's sister. "Hi, Lisa, I've been hoping you would call. Are you joining us tomorrow for dinner?"

Lisa's voice sounded like she was on speakerphone. "I'm heading your way now. Doug is stuck on call through the weekend, but he'll have dinner tomorrow with his family. I was hoping I could stay at Nana's house with you. Leah said you were there by yourself while Nana is in the hospital."

"I'd be thrilled to have the company. How far out are you?" I'd stopped trying to haul stuff inside and talk on the phone simultaneously, so I sat down on the steps outside the kitchen.

"I'll be there in about ninety minutes. I just got through Alexandria. Are you sure you don't mind? Leah asked me to stay with them, but I wanted you and I to catch up since we didn't get a lot of time to chat during Karen's wedding."

I snorted. "It was a vow-renewal ceremony, but I can see how *wedding* seems a more fitting description."

"Oh, it was a wedding all right. Vow renewals don't often have multiple bridesmaids dressed in purple like that." Lisa was funny once you got to know her, and she had this great Cajun accent that my Cypress Bayou family didn't.

"Those purple dresses were the worst for sure. I'm thrilled you're coming here now. You can help me brine the hundred-pound turkey I bought. Well, it's not quite that big, but twenty pounds at least."

Lisa laughed. "There are a lot of them to feed for sure. Okay, I'll see you soon then."

"Drive safely."

Karen arrived, but I didn't tell her about Lisa's arriving tonight. My hope was to work with Karen to get the table set before Lisa arrived.

"So, for Thanksgiving, we use this pattern." We stood in front of the china cabinet in the dining room where a huge number of dishes lived. "And these glasses."

"There are so many. How do you keep it all straight?" I murmured.

"I've been setting the table for Momma my whole life. I know all the patterns by heart." There were at least four or five complete place settings. "Oh, we use these for Christmas." She pointed to what I recognized as Limoges. My mom had had a setting of four and they'd been her prized possession. I had them packed in a box that I'd moved from Chicago because I couldn't bear to part with them.

"The tablecloths are in here." She bent down to where the drawers were. "Momma has them dry-cleaned after every holiday and stores them in each drawer. This is the one we use for Thanksgiving. Oh, and the napkins and rings are here."

"I just brought in the groceries when you arrived, so I'll let you get started while I put things away."

By the time I'd sorted the kitchen, leaving out the items I would use tonight, Karen was nearly done with her dining table. "Wow, that was fast, and it looks amazing."

She shrugged her shoulders, accepting my compliment.

"I'm just so glad you're here with us for the holidays this year."

"Me too."

NICK STOPPED BY his parents' house before heading upstairs to his apartment. "Oh, I'm glad you're here, honey. I need you to go up and grab Thomas the Turkey from the attic." And so, it began. His mom pointing, and him doing her bidding as she prepped for Thanksgiving tomorrow.

"I don't know why you go to such trouble for only the three of us. You'll cook all morning, and we'll eat everything in twenty minutes," Nick grumbled as he wrestled the ceramic turkey that had graced the center of his mother's Thanksgiving Day feast since he was a little boy. In fact, he couldn't remember a Thanksgiving where the wonky-eyed gobbler hadn't stared him down as he inhaled turkey and dressing.

"I can't believe you still have this thing," Nick said as he placed the giant, garishly painted fowl in his place of honor, dead center on the white tablecloth.

"Are you kidding? It wouldn't be Thanksgiving without him." His mother patted Thomas the Turkey.

"I'm going to head up now, Mom."

"Okay. I think that's everything." She stood, hands on hips in front of the naked turkey still defrosting in the sink—who would be their main course tomorrow. She turned toward Nick and asked, "Oh, have you heard anything about Elise today? I've been so busy that I haven't taken a minute to check in on her condition."

"As of last night, she was showing signs of improvement, but I haven't gotten an update since."

His mom's eyebrows went up. "Were you with Allison last night?"

"I was." Nick didn't update his mother on his daily actions unless she asked. But he wasn't about to fill in any unnecessary details or she would never give him peace.

"Does she want children?"

It took Nick a second to comprehend her question. "What are you talking about? Why would you ask me that?"

"You want a family, Nick. You always have. Before you get serious with this girl, you'd better find out if she envisions the same things in her future. I know you see me as a busybody, but I'm on your side, son, and I want you to be happy above all things."

Nick was uncertain how to respond to that. "I know you do, Mom. But you need to let me work out my own relationships."

His mother nodded. "I just thought it was something you should think about."

"When I'm ready to think about it, I'll ask the right questions, okay?"

"All right, fine. I'll leave it alone for now. But you should bring her to dinner soon so we can get to know her."

"I'll keep you posted." He left her and went up to his place, still fuming about his mother's need to interfere in his life. It was time he thought about getting a place that wasn't within walking distance to his parents.

But his mom's words crept up on him as he grabbed a

beer from the fridge and plopped down on his sofa. *Does Allison want children?* He didn't think age had much to do with it. Lots of couples their age had babies. But was that in her life's plan? They hadn't spoken about it—hadn't even mentioned it since they'd met.

"I'M SO GLAD you came tonight." I greeted Lisa on the front porch steps. By then, Karen was long gone, having gotten the table set in record time.

"I'm a little ragged, but glad to be out of the car. There was a lot of traffic on I-49, so I was on high alert the entire time."

We had a quick hug and I asked, "Do you need help brining anything inside?"

"Nope. I'll only be here a couple of days, so I packed light—well, light for me." She carried a large duffel and a hanging bag. "How's Nana doing?"

"Today they got her heart back into rhythm, so she's coming along. She has a slight paralysis on her left side from her first stroke, but they've gotten her up with the physical therapist assisting, and she's even walking a little using a walker. Her speech is a bit garbled, but all her vitals are stable and strong, according to Jake."

"Yes, I spoke with him a couple of days ago and then with Leah, but I didn't know if anything had changed."

"She is making remarkable progress." I'd been thrilled to hear the good news today about Nana's heart.

Lisa smiled. "This family loves her so much. I'd hate it if

they'd lost her—if you'd lost her."

I had to agree with that. We'd entered the house as we talked, and I showed her to her room upstairs. "Thanks, Allison. I'll wash my hands and we can get busy brining that big bird."

As proper as Lisa usually dressed and behaved, she was a great cook and didn't mind getting her hands dirty. So many people here in Louisiana were natural-born cooks. I guess I should take more of an interest.

Lisa met me in the kitchen wearing a sweatshirt with her jeans. "Wow, I've never seen you so casual."

She laughed at that. "I'll admit that I do like nice clothes but when I'm home and not planning to go out, this is how I look."

"Okay, maybe I'm not quite as intimidated now." Lisa was a class act and I sometimes wondered how she managed to seem so put together all the time.

"Oh, stop." Lisa laughed at my backhanded compliment.

We set to work by cleaning out the inside of the bird. "It's a good thing Nana has this huge sink, or we'd be in trouble." I reached inside the cavity and realized the innards were packed neatly inside a mesh bag, which I pulled out. Lisa wrinkled her nose at what was inside.

"Where are we going to put this thing overnight?" she asked. "I don't think there's room in that refrigerator." Lisa nodded toward the large stainless fridge.

"The internet suggests a cooler with ice-water brine, so it stays cold enough if it won't fit inside. There's a huge one out in the garage."

We worked and chatted for almost an hour, deciding to

place the turkey inside Nana's biggest gumbo pot filled with Lisa's recipe for the brining solution of water, coarse salt, brown sugar, and a little wine vinegar. I would've used salt and water only, how my mom had, but Lisa's sounded way better.

"The outside freezer should have a couple of bags of ice." We placed the giant pot inside the giant cooler and surrounded it with ice.

"Whew. That was a big job. I'm so glad you were here to help."

"Me too." The front of Lisa's shirt had evidence of our exertion. "Let me go change my clothes and we can relax."

"Okay, I'll pour some wine. Cabernet okay?" I asked.

"Perfect."

By the time Lisa came back down, she was wearing a matched set of long-sleeved pajamas with candy canes on them.

She caught my amused look. "What? Too soon?"

"Christmas Festival is in just over a week, so I guess it's not too soon. Plus, anything Christmassy after Thanksgiving is in season. We'll ignore that you're a day early."

"Thanks for giving me a little grace."

I lifted my glass in salute. "You bet."

We settled in the family room in matching club chairs and put our feet up on the matching ottomans. "Ah, this is nice. So, tell me about things here. Are you settling in? Anything I need to know about?" Lisa asked.

I didn't know where to begin, honestly. "Well, people are still staring at me everywhere I go, but they aren't actually pointing anymore, so that's progress, I guess."

"Oh, these small towns are pretty much all the same in that regard. Doug is from New Iberia, and they still point at me when we go to visit his parents. Anybody new gets the full treatment."

"I'm getting used to how things roll here. The town is lovely, but being the talk of the town, not so much." I took a sip of my wine. "I've been seeing a nice guy since I arrived. His name is Nick."

"Nick the mechanic?"

"Yes. Do you know him?"

"I met him while I was staying here in town trying to find my grandmother. Very cute, Allison. He changed the oil in my car and Carly introduced him as a close family friend. So, that's convenient. The family knows him and already approves. Saves a couple steps, actually."

"The family knows everyone, but yes, they seem to have a special fondness for Nick. My problem is that I don't know for sure what my plans are long term. I've got a list on the fridge at my apartment with the pros and cons of moving here—and staying here permanently. I keep adding to both sides, so it's not helping much."

"I don't think you should base this decision on a list, Allison. You have to feel it in your heart before you can make that decision. I know that you've lived most of your life without knowing your birth family. I've lived most of mine not knowing the circumstances of my birth or how I came to be a daughter to people who were complicit in covering up my birth mother's death to save their own skin. That has taken some real soul searching and therapy to find forgiveness for my adoptive parents, let me tell you."

"I guess it would. My issue was being given up in a closed adoption, and knowing my family didn't ever want me to find them or them to find me someday. I felt thrown away, honestly."

"I get it. People do things that are incomprehensible. But when I think of who I was in my teens and who I am now, I cringe at some of the decisions I made then out of ignorance and innocence. The Bertrands were so thrilled to find you and it's obvious how much they want you in their lives."

"I believe that, I do, but sometimes I don't know where I fit in this family."

"I do the same thing, wondering if I can ever find peace after everything that's happened. My grandmother has helped a lot. Watching her show forgiveness to my parents after their part in my birth mom's disappearance has been incredible. She's done it for me, so that I can feel better about things." Lisa's grandmother was Marie Trichel, the woman whom the judge and Carson Carmichael—who turned out to be her dad—had had committed as insane.

"I guess it's about forgiveness and moving forward, huh?" I'd known this but I hadn't actually let it sink in until I heard Lisa's story, which admittedly was way more unbelievable than mine.

"You said it, sister." We clinked our glasses.

"I know the family will be happy you came to be with us tomorrow." Lisa had bonded with the Bertrands immediately and I kind of envied her that ease of acceptance.

"I needed to see my brothers and to check on Nana. I'd like to visit her at the hospital before I leave."

"Yes, it's been a couple of days since I've gone over. She's been in the ICU until today, so it's been a bit tough to see her."

Lisa yawned. "I guess I'd better go to bed so I can be up and ready to help with dinner in the morning—and I'll need the energy to face everyone."

"Yes, I need rest to sidestep Karen's incessant urge to corner me."

"Karen is one of a kind, for sure."

We turned off the lights and I double-checked the doors before we went upstairs to bed.

CHAPTER TWENTY-TWO

I PUT ON classic Christmas carols on the television as background music while we made stuffing and wrestled the turkey, who'd grown substantially larger overnight due to it absorbing the brining solution.

"This thing is a monster," Lisa grunted as we lifted the big bird into the enormous roasting pan. I'd bought an extra-large roasting bag to cook it in.

I removed all but the bottom rack in the oven so it would fit inside. But we first had to stuff the cavity with the cornbread stuffing we'd made. I'd decided that the herbed recipe Mom and I had always used might not be something everybody here liked, so early this morning, I made several pans of cornbread to use in the concoction. Lisa was an old pro with cornbread *dressing*—they called it here.

"Is it going to be too dry?" I wondered as we chopped onions and celery, sauteed them with spices, and then mixed it up with the crumbled cornbread and raw egg, butter, and chicken stock.

"When the juices from the turkey release into the stuffing, it will add a lot of moisture, so don't worry about it being too dry," Lisa said as she shoved another handful of the mixture into the bird's opening.

Lisa and I laughed at our antics, and I realized that I

hadn't had this much fun with another woman since I'd been here. "I'm really glad you're here." I enjoyed my sisters' company, but Lisa was a real *hoot*. It was a new local word I'd picked up, and it suited her perfectly.

"Me too. I would hug you, but my hands are full of stuff you don't want on your shirt." We both laughed when she wiggled her goopy fingers.

Being here with someone who truly understood my situation had calmed some of my raw edges and bonded us even more. Not only did she understand me, but I also understood her.

We finally got the stuffed turkey in the oven and cleaned the substantial mess we'd created in the process. "Okay, this is going to take at least five hours. What time did you say they were coming over?" Lisa asked.

"In about four hours, around noon, so we can shower and get things together in the meantime. And maybe watch a movie before they arrive."

"Sounds good."

"Smells amazing in here. I'm starving." Jake entered the kitchen, gave Lisa a hug, and then hugged me. He deposited a huge bowl of mashed potatoes next to the pecan streusel pie cooling on the countertop. He then peered through the oven door at our turkey that was browning nicely in the roasting bag.

"You'll have to wait one more hour, according to the instructions." Lisa and I were organizing ice and glasses. I'd lined up some canned sodas on the countertop. "Hey, can you fill those with ice and water?" I pointed to the gorgeous crystal pitchers I'd found in the bottom of the china cabinet.

"Sure thing." Jake set to work.

Leah came in carrying a pan of brownies and a couple of bottles of wine. "We'll need these, y'all. Happy Thanksgiving. It's great to see you, Lisa."

Before Lisa could reply, Karen and Bob burst into the room with three casserole dishes between them. "I made my famous dressing. Just wait until you taste it."

My stomach sank. Hadn't she heard I was making the stuffing? I didn't want to say anything about it yet. The last thing we all needed was for Karen to feel like her dressing was in competition with my stuffing. Or maybe she'd done it on purpose? This group could probably polish off both, so hopefully it would be fine.

Carly and Tanner arrived with a pan of sweet potato casserole and a couple of dozen deviled eggs. "Mmm, I can smell the cinnamon in that." Lisa sniffed. "That's my favorite Thanksgiving food."

Carly and Tanner greeted Lisa. "We're glad you made it. Sorry Doug couldn't make it."

"Yeah. Me too."

"Can we help with anything? Turkey smells fantastic, Allison."

"Thanks. It was a team effort to wrestle that gigantic bird into the oven."

Tanner glanced into the oven. "Wow, that's quite a beast."

"Mind if we change the channel to football?" Bob stuck

his head in the doorway and gestured toward the living room.

"Of course."

Karen entered the kitchen and tapped a spoon against one of the crystal glasses. "Great news, everybody! I just got a call from the hospital and if everything goes well, Momma will get to come home tomorrow. She's declined going to inpatient rehab, but a physical therapist can come here to the house to do it."

A cheer went up in the house. Relief flooded through me at hearing this. "I'll stay here with her as long as she needs someone. Lydia has offered for me to work from home so I can help Nana."

"How kind of you, Allison. Thanks for staying here while she's been away." Karen patted my shoulder.

"It's been my pleasure."

It was as if someone had let the pressure out of the house. The relief that Nana would come home tomorrow was palpable. Leah uncorked the wine and poured everyone a glass who wanted one.

Tanner and Jake took the turkey from the oven when the timer sounded, and Jake did the carving. Everyone gathered the food and carried it to the enormous dining room table. I wondered if it would all fit, including the platter of turkey.

Bob stood then and said, "I'm sad Nana's not here but at least she's headed home. To Nana."

"To Nana!" We all raised our glasses in toast to the woman who was the family glue.

"Well, I have to say that I'll be interested to try your dressing. I thought everybody knew that I *always* bring the cornbread dressing." Karen carefully spooned a tiny portion of my stuffing onto her plate.

Leah frowned at Karen's insinuation that she'd been slighted. So, Leah scooped a big spoon of my stuffing onto her plate. "Looks amazing, Allison."

Carly did the same, causing Karen to make a frustrated harrumphing noise.

I absorbed the complete support from my sisters. I got that this is how they taught our mother a lesson, but why didn't just somebody tell me not to make the stuffing? So, to calm Karen's frazzled nerves, I helped myself to a serving of her dressing and took a bite. "Mmm, delicious. You'll have to tell me how you make it."

I noticed an approving glance from Bob. I hated that every time there was discord involving Karen, he was the one who had to deal with the fallout. Poor guy deserved a reward.

Karen preened at my praise. "Of course, I'll give you some pointers, dear. Yours isn't bad though."

"Lisa and I made it together."

The sounds of silverware scraping china was predominant for the next half an hour. "Dessert anyone?" I asked as soon as we were all done eating.

"I wish I could put one more thing in my stomach right now," Carly groaned. "Give me thirty minutes and I'll be all over that pumpkin pie."

"Oh, and don't forget my Jell-O salad," Karen reminded them.

I had to ask what the ingredients were before I dug into the frothy mint-green concoction. I'd heard rumors about carrots and other kinds of odd items people sometimes mixed in.

"Well, there's green Jell-O, 7Up, cherries, crushed pineapple, Cool Whip, and cream cheese." Karen listed the ingredients by heart.

"Sounds yummy."

"Leah likes it, but Carly won't touch it. You'll be our deciding vote." Karen raised her eyebrows to gauge my reaction.

"It's good. Different than I'm used to, but fluffy and sweet."

Karen nodded in satisfaction as I noticed Carly making a gagging motion with her finger, which caused me to snort with laughter unexpectedly.

After dessert, everyone cleaned and helped to restore Nana's kitchen before heading into the family room to watch football, visit, and nap.

WE MANAGED TO get Nana settled in the downstairs bedroom of her house. She grumbled a little about all the "fuss" as she called it.

Nick would arrive at my apartment soon, so I wanted to get there before him and make a fresh pot of coffee as fuel for our labors. But first, I parked next to the curb in front of my place and walked down the sidewalk to the bakery to pick up a half dozen croissants and some fresh fruit. I could bring what I didn't eat to Nana later.

I sat outside on my balcony at the tiny table drinking

coffee and inhaling a cinnamon scent. I couldn't tell if it was coming from downstairs or just wafting by from the bakery where I'd stopped and grabbed breakfast. Either way, I peered out at all the symbols of Christmas as far as the eye could see, and the delicious scent added to the festive atmosphere.

I took a deep breath and exhaled. Saturday mornings were the best, and I had to admit, between the nice weather, the view of the bayou with all its merry décor, and the cinnamon, I had a sudden urge to put on Christmas music. I almost couldn't remember the last time that had happened—certainly not in the past couple of years as I'd struggled to deal with my mom's death and my cancer. So yeah, my Christmas spirit hadn't exactly been at an all-time high. But I was better now from all that, and my enthusiasm was inching back, thanks to my new surroundings and the people in my life.

I planned to take this decision on whether or not to stay permanently in Cypress Bayou a day at a time with the help of my ever-evolving list of pros and cons.

I admired Nick's form as he pulled out what appeared to be a ladder and toolbelt. I had a little thing for guys in toolbelts, admittedly. And he wore one well.

"YOU LOOK PRETTY comfy up there." He shielded his eyes from the sun with his hand as he peered up to where Allison sat.

"I am. Come on up and I'll feed you a croissant and a

cup of coffee before I work you half to death."

"Sounds like a good trade-off." Nick opened the gate as soon as he heard the buzzer that permitted him onto the stairwell.

She opened the door so he could enter. "Hi there."

"You said something about coffee and pastries?" He couldn't help grinning at her.

"Sure did. Follow me." Allison led them toward the kitchen.

"The place looks great." He noticed a few small Christmas items and a red throw on the sofa.

"I haven't had much time to decorate for myself since I arrived." She said this with a quirk of her lips.

"People around here like to set out their *predicaments* on the front porch and let 'em wave at the neighbors. Not a lot of hiding the crazy, if you know what I mean." He was referencing all the drama in Cypress Bayou the past year or so. "So, making a good joke here and there about your recent predicament feels healthy to me."

"I'm a living, breathing *predicament* around here. A decades-old shocking *predicament* in this town."

He laughed at the parallel she'd drawn. "Yes. Like you. But you've turned out to be the best-kept secret I know."

They both laughed. "I guess I'm interesting, at least for now."

"Don't worry, while you'll always be interesting, they'll move on to the next big shocking predicament that rolls in and start treating you like you're just one of the folks."

"Do you think it'll ever get to that point for me? I want to believe that I'll soon be yesterday's news so that I won't get stared at and whispered about everywhere I go."

An idea occurred to Nick. "Hmm. I think I might know a way to speed up that process."

"I'm all ears here."

"What if you hosted a holiday drop-in for the locals here at the loft? Spread it over a few days during Christmas Festival weekend. Meet everyone and talk to them. Do a little networking. Let them see you as one of the Bertrand family instead of only getting a glimpse of you around town?"

Allison frowned. "That idea rates up there with my worst nightmare. I mean, inviting strangers into my home?" She shuddered.

"Think about it. Once their curiosity is satisfied, they'll see you as one of them—us. I know it's out of your comfort zone, but that weekend is historically when we get together here in town and celebrate the beginning of the Christmas season. Your family comes to this apartment every year and spends time with friends. You'd already planned to host an open house on festival weekend, right? So, we get the word out to people that this is an open house to locals, hosted by you and the Bertrands."

"I'm not sure. I'm not afraid to do it, I just don't know if they'll like me."

"Ha. What's not to like?" His reply came out so easily, so he hoped she heard the truth in his words.

"I'll discuss it with my family and see what they think of the idea. With Nana still recovering, I'm not sure."

"I think Nana would approve. In fact, if she were here, she would sit right there on the balcony and reign over the whole thing. She's the backbone of this place. People look to her for her advice and opinion."

"She does seem to be popular."

"Yes, she is. You know she hosts a gigantic crawfish boil every year to raise money for charity, right? Almost everybody in town attends and she opens up Plaisance House for tours the week before the party."

"I remember still being in Cypress General during the big event. Bob even brought by a container of boiled crawfish and showed me how to peel and eat the tails. He tried to describe the party to me, and it sounded like great fun."

"I didn't realize you were in town last year during the crawfish boil." Nick thought about her sitting in her hospital room alone and it made him a little sad to imagine.

"Don't worry, I'll be there this year and eat my weight in crawfish to celebrate."

"I can't wait to see that." He laughed, remembering her first oyster.

"Okay, let's get started here."

"We can get the exterior done today and you can worry about the inside later, after you come back from Nana's and have more time." Allison had shared with him yesterday that she was planning to bring her work for Lydia home to Nana's house during her recovery, which he thought was a fantastic idea.

Together, they hauled all the greenery and a huge plastic tub of assorted Christmas accessories upstairs to Allison's apartment. His admiration for her creativity blossomed as she assembled a gorgeous, multi-tiered garland, using lights, bows, and strands of gold beads and flowers. "Wow, I feel sorry for the other folks. Theirs isn't nearly as nice." He looked on one side, then the other.

"Mine is supposed to look professional because it is."

"What do you have planned for downstairs?" he asked while she continued to tweak things on the balcony.

"I need to get the keys from Mrs. Sibley so I can tear down the butcher paper and hang some fabric a little farther back, so we have room to decorate the display windows on both sides. That way, nobody will see the interior, but the front will be festive."

"Sounds like you've worked it all out in your head already."

She turned toward Nick, her smile infectious. "I've been thinking about it since I moved in."

"How about you let me go and grab the keys from Mrs. Sibley, and you finish up here?"

"Sounds perfect. But if you're not careful, you'll be staying for tea."

Nick nodded in agreement. "I'll have to promise to come by next week."

"You're a good guy, Nick Landry."

NICK LEFT TO get the keys from Mrs. Sibley while I tweaked things on the balcony. Satisfied with our work thus far, I stepped inside and checked my phone to see if anyone had left a message. I breathed a sigh of relief that I wasn't needed anywhere at the moment. I wanted to finish this project today, and this would give me time to do that.

Nick returned with the keys for downstairs. While he was gone, I'd gathered up the items I would need to do the job. "Got it. And Mrs. Sibley said to tell you thanks and feel free to do whatever you want. She's relieved that her empty space won't be a blight on the neighborhood."

"A blight?" I laughed at the wording, but I understood her meaning. I felt the same and would try to do her proud.

"That's a direct quote from the lady herself." He pointed toward the large tub of accessories I'd planned to add to the window treatment. "This stuff going downstairs with us?"

"Yes, please. We can make one trip down with this stuff and then come back up for the greenery we didn't use up here."

"You head downstairs, and I'll bring everything there. I'm here to work, you know?" He handed me the keys and I headed downstairs with a stapler, a pair of scissors, and my phone in hand.

As I propped open the front doors, I was hit with the cinnamon smell I'd been enjoying since that morning. It was like a welcome home.

"Wow, it smells like Christmas in here." Nick inhaled the spicy scent as he plopped down the tub. "It's like this place has a mind of its own."

I'd thought the same thing several times since I'd lived here, but it was reassuring instead of concerning. "So long as the next smell isn't two-day-old garbage."

"Ha. Let's hope not."

Nick helped me tack the shimmery silver fabric to the top of the window casement about five feet back from the glass, creating a background that hung almost to the floor.

We pulled off the butcher paper carefully, as it was a little dusty, and rolled it up.

The glass was cleaner than I expected it would be considering the amount of time it had been covered. I would use some spray cleaner on the outside later. I quickly worked to hang the dozen or more cartoonishly large and colorful ornaments I'd found in Lydia's storeroom and then draped the lit garland to frame the window. I added faux snow at the bottom and decided to use the set of smallish silver trees at different heights. It wasn't super fancy, but it was festive and colorful with a flair for the dramatic.

"Let's see if these work." Nick plugged the heavy extension cord into a small surge suppressor I'd brought over. The colorful lights bounced off the sparkling fabric, bringing the entire window to life. "Wow. It looks fantastic."

"Not bad, huh? Let's see if the window spotlights work. We might need some new bulbs." I found the electric panel in back and flipped the switch marked *front window*.

"They're on!" Nick called from up front.

The effect was nearly magical with the whole thing lit up, and I was satisfied with the result for so little time spent on the project. "You're so talented," Nick said surveying the finished window.

A couple of car honks in passing caused Nick to look up and wave. "I guess standing in the window in plain sight must've gotten us recognized." He bent down and picked up a couple of loose needles that had fallen from the garland.

We cleaned up our mess and locked the doors, and as I stared up at my lovely balcony and then at the space below, I got a sudden picture of myself living and working here. It surprised me that I could see it so clearly. "You okay?"

I nodded and smiled but didn't share my thoughts.

He helped me load my car with items we'd not used so I could bring them back to Lydia. She was in the store, so I decided to make a quick stop and unload the items so I could replace them with the supplies to bring home to work on.

Nick insisted on helping, so it was done in less than half the time it would have taken me to make trips back and forth to the car.

"Can I buy you lunch?" he asked when we were finished.

I checked the time on my phone. "Well, technically, I owe *you* lunch but I'll have to give you a rain check. I need to get back to Nana's."

CHAPTER TWENTY-THREE

LISA WAS PACKING up to head back to South Louisiana, which made me a little sad. "I've enjoyed spending time together. I hate to see you go back so soon."

"I had a lovely time with y'all, but my sweet husband has gotten some great last-minute LSU vs. Texas A&M tickets for this weekend and wants me to go to the game with him."

"Enjoy the game." I'd never been to a college football game in my life, but they appeared on TV to be lots of fun.

Lisa shut the trunk of her car and turned to me. "Call me anytime, Allison. I'm here for you, okay?" We hugged and I almost teared up.

"Thanks for coming and helping me. I had a blast."

"Me too."

I stood on Nana's front porch as she drove away, and just as I turned to go inside, my phone vibrated in my back pocket.

It was Elizabeth.

"Okay, we forgive you for missing Thanksgiving dinner yesterday because I know you were needed by the Bertrands. I called because you and I need to go Christmas shopping in Shreveport. It's almost Christmas Festival and you'll need a new dress for our holiday party. My treat." I don't think she'd even taken a breath before spitting out all those words.

It took me a second to comprehend it all. "Hi, Elizabeth. Sorry about dinner. I promised Tootie I'd stop by this weekend sometime."

"And shopping? How about next weekend? My schedule is pretty light and I'm not on call Saturday or Sunday. The next weekend is Christmas Festival, so that's not a good time."

"I'm working at least a half of a day on Saturday, so yeah, Sunday works."

"Sunday it is. So, I'm not telling Momma that we're going until afterward because she might want to tag along. The woman doesn't need a single thing, so there's no point in her going except to annoy you—or annoy us both."

"O-okay." I didn't have a response to that, but I got her drift. Tootie Keller could be a lot.

"I've decided that we should do things like lunch and shopping together. I mean, I've forgiven Daddy for being such an idiot where your poor pregnant momma was concerned, so there's no reason for us not to try out this sister thing for real."

"I'd like that, Elizabeth. Thanks for reaching out." I realized I was smiling then.

"Well, I've got some making up to do. I didn't react well to finding out about you at first. And the whole Jake and Leah thing was a pretty huge blow to me. A real loss of my unrealistic plans for the future."

"I don't hold any of that against you. I'm sorry you were disappointed."

"Believe me, I've had to work on myself the past year to finally get over Jake. I thought he was the only one I could love and that if I didn't have him, there'd be nobody for me. It's taken a while to come to grips that he's always loved Leah. I know people think I'm still hung up on him, but I'm not. I'm finally free of that terrible kind of love."

"I'm glad to hear that you're moving on. It's a big step." I was shocked that Elizabeth had confided in me about what happened with Jake. It sounded like she'd gotten some real perspective lately.

"Well, I might be tired of being the most hated woman in town. It's pretty lonely, you know?"

"I'm certain you aren't hated, Elizabeth. You've known these people your entire life, and even if they don't view you as a good friend, you're part of this town. Besides, how many of their lives have you saved?"

Elizabeth barked a laugh. "I honestly hadn't thought about it like that. I guess they'd better be nice to me, huh? Never know when somebody might need a heart surgeon."

"And they could be just a little jealous of your accomplishments—oh, and all those *shoes*."

"It's true. My shoes are killer. And yours will be too if you listen to me. I'll text you next week to work out details. It'll be fun."

"Yes, I think it will. Thanks for inviting me."

After I hung up with Elizabeth, I continued to smile. I guess I'd have to add her to the plus column after all. If I wasn't careful, I wouldn't have any reason not to stay here.

NANA, KAREN, CARLY, and I piled up in Nana's room and

watched three episodes of Nana's favorite show about some city folks getting stuck in a small town. I had to say there were some parts I resonated strongly with. But it was a comedy, so it was a funny kind of truth.

After, we decided to order pizza for dinner, which was something I hadn't done since moving here. Somehow Louisiana made even pizza with shrimp and crawfish. "Oh, wow, this is fantastic." I said this between bites.

"Are you a New York-style or Chicago-style pizza fan?" Carly asked me.

"Both. I like a thin crust for some kinds, but I get in the mood for deep-dish like I grew up with. I guess there's no going wrong with good pizza."

"Amen to that, my girl." I tried not to bristle when Karen called me her girl. I mean, it was nice to hang with these women who were my blood kin, but something about the way Karen took every advantage to claim me still rubbed me wrong.

We'd helped Nana into the kitchen once the pizza arrived and were all currently sitting around the table working our way through two large pizzas. One was shrimp and sausage and the other a mash-up of crawfish and cheese. I'd skipped lunch and my croissant from this morning was just a happy memory.

"So, Allison, we haven't talked lately about you and Nick. What's up with the two of you?" Nana looked so much like herself that if I didn't know she'd had a stroke, I wouldn't be able to tell.

But I didn't love her question, even though it was a legitimate one. "Mmm. Not sure what to say. I like him but I don't want to get too involved if I decide not to stay in Cypress Bayou, you know?" That was my mantra, and I was sticking to it.

"Why on earth wouldn't you want to stay here with us?" Karen asked with a slight whine as if this was unpleasant and possibly shocking news to her.

I wanted to say: because of that right there. But instead, I said, "I miss Chicago, you know? I know that none of you have spent time there, but it's my home, and it's the only link I have to my mom." And this was all true.

"But she's not there anymore, sweetheart. I don't want to sound unkind, but we're the only family you have. Give us a chance." Karen sounded forlorn.

"Stop. We can't tell Allison what she should do with her life, no matter how much we'd like for her to stay." Nana's lips were almost keeping up with her words, and I could tell she was struggling to speak smoothly.

"Thanks, Nana. There are days when I'm still not sure I can fit in here." Thanksgiving had been such a nice time with them all, it was getting hard to imagine living far away again.

Nana nodded and caught me in her stare. "I'm removing the stipulation on your trust fund. I don't want your decision to be clouded in any way, so first thing Monday morning, I'm calling the bank and releasing the funds to you. That way, you can leave if you feel it's necessary."

I was stunned. "You don't have to do that, Nana. I owe you the year after all you've done for me."

She waved a hand as if swatting at a fly. "No. I've changed my mind, which I don't do often, m'dear. Having this stroke has taught me that life is short, and it was a selfish act of an old woman trying to control things. You don't owe any of us anything. I should've given you the money free and clear the moment we found out you were looking for us. It was manipulative and I'm sorry."

There was dead silence in the room, and I hesitated to look at each of their faces. "I agree with you, Nana. Allison shouldn't have to make her decision like that." Carly put a hand on my shoulder.

Karen, for once, said nothing.

I didn't know what to say or to think. Nana's words tossed me into confusion, like she'd changed the rules of the game right in the middle of play. Did Nana not want me here now that she'd gotten to know me? I know that sounded childish, but it threw me. I just couldn't figure out this sudden change in the stakes.

I found my voice then. "Are you kicking me out? I don't understand." I'd had all the power before now, I realized. Yes, Nana had pulled the strings with her money, but my decision to stay or go was mine entirely, and if I left, it would be with the money after a year.

Nana's eye filled with tears. "No, dear. Of course not. But I don't want to hold you back either. The best part of your life is still ahead of you, and if being here is keeping you from that, then I want to allow you all the advantages to pursue your dreams."

"Thank you for everything you've done for me." To avoid showing them weakness, I stood with my plate and walked into the kitchen. I tried hard to control the tears that had gathered in my eyes. This still felt like a rejection. Like them telling me they didn't care whether I stayed or not.

"I'm going to head up to bed. I'll see you in the morning, Nana. Let me know if you need anything during the night." Carly and Karen's expressions were grim, and Nana's appeared vulnerable.

I stayed stalwart until I got halfway up the stairs. I shut the door to my room and threw myself on the bed, trying to stifle the sobs. I hadn't cried since my mom died. I hated to cry, to show weakness in front of anyone. But I cried now. For Mom, for the loss of these amazing women and Bob. Nick. And even Elizabeth. It suddenly occurred to me that I couldn't leave any of them. Certainly not yet.

There was a soft knock at my door and Carly asked, "Can I come in?"

"Um. Okay." I swiped at my face, trying to pretend I hadn't been sobbing only seconds before.

Carly shut the door and came over to me and sat down on the bed. "Oh, honey. I think you misunderstood Nana."

"It felt like a dismissal. Like the experiment is over." My lip quivered again.

"No. No. No. She believed she was being manipulative and asking too much from you, expecting you to stay here if you didn't want to. We *want* you here, Allison. You are our missing puzzle piece. And nobody is expecting you to trust us all or accept us as your family overnight, or even in one year." Carly drew me into a tight hug. "I can't imagine how alone you've felt since your mom died. We are here for you."

I let out a ragged sigh. "I've been so lost."

Carly pulled back but took my hands in hers. "Well, you have to decide what you want from your life. We're just supporting cast here. What are your dreams, Allison?"

It hit me with clarity then, how all of this had lined up. "I think I'd like to open a business here in Cypress Bayou."

Carly grinned, obviously surprised. "You do? What kind of business?"

"An interiors and accessories shop in the old soap store."

Carly's eyes sparkled with excitement. "What a great idea! How can I help with your dream?"

"You've already done so much. All of you have."

"Nonsense. I want to be your sister and so does Leah—in a meaningful way. And sisters stick up for each other. They annoy, tease, and support each other."

Her honest response warmed my heart. "I-I don't know what to say. I would welcome your ideas and suggestions as to what would work in a town like this."

"Let's go to the soap store tomorrow afternoon and have a look. Leah is coming back from New Orleans early tomorrow, so we can all go together. You can talk out your ideas with Leah, and we can all put our heads together to help make it a reality. This is so exciting, Allison."

My world had turned a little sunnier all of a sudden. I knew where I wanted to be—finally. I had ideas and dreams I was too afraid to chase until now. The scales had tipped in the favor of Cypress Bayou in a consequential way.

CHAPTER TWENTY-FOUR

NICK STOPPED IN at his parents' house after changing the brake pads and oil in his truck at the shop. Currently, his dad was watching football in the keeping room off the kitchen, and Nick thought he might join him. He assumed Allison was with her family.

His mom was sitting out on her screened porch reading a novel. She looked up at him over her glasses when he entered the room. "Well, hello, son. Haven't seen you but coming and going for a few days. I've got some fried chicken and mashed potatoes still warm in the oven if you're hungry."

He gave his mother a grateful glance. "I couldn't pass up your homemade fried chicken even if I wasn't hungry, Mom."

"We went to church at ten this morning, so I made a late lunch. Saw Karen and Bob there. Karen says you're still spending a lot of time with Allison."

"I see Allison sometimes. She's been staying at her nana's house since the second stroke." He chose his words carefully, not wanting to get into a big discussion about his personal life. "But I'd heard she came home from the hospital."

"I'm glad for that." His mother's eyes were shrewd. "Do you know what you want with Allison?"

He frowned. "I want Allison to stay in Cypress Bayou.

Beyond that, we'll see."

"You mean she's not staying?" He heard a thread of hope in her voice.

"I don't know if she's staying. She's trying to decide." He shifted on his feet, uncomfortable with her line of questioning. "I can't tell her what she should do. I can only wait to see what she decides."

"Sounds like you're frustrated." His mom's gaze was speculative.

"Maybe a little." He felt like he'd been following Allison around like a heartsick puppy. It was humbling to say the least. "So, I'll go and see about that fried chicken."

"There's pie in the fridge. Chocolate," she called as he exited the room.

As he pulled the leftovers from the oven, Nick was overcome with a sense of helplessness. He couldn't change the situation by being impatient with Allison. And he did understand her needing time to decide the course of her future. His life and his future had always seemed like a clear path. He would stay here in Cypress Bayou, run the family business, and take care of his parents when needed.

As far as his love life, well, that hadn't been so clear. He'd had a couple disastrous relationships and a few disappointments, aside from dating Izzy when they were younger. At thirty-five, he figured it was time to chart a course toward what he wanted: a wife and a family.

He wondered if Allison would leave him hanging for long. Even if she stayed, would she want to be with him? Unfortunately for Nick, she'd been the first woman who'd struck him as someone he could see himself with in the future. With the other women, he'd been blinded by things that didn't matter. And by the time he'd figured that out, he'd developed more baggage, including the inability to trust women at their word.

Allison was gorgeous, yes, but it was her ability to see him as a person and not what he could offer her that attracted him the most. She was careful with her emotions, but she had no guile. She'd been honest and hadn't led him on.

THE IDEA THAT you don't get to pick your family rang true for me. Finding the Bertrands, and now, Lisa, when I had probably saved my life in more than one way. There were far from perfect as a whole. In fact, I'd say that Karen was exasperating even. But collectively they had lifted me from illness and grief and cared for me when they hadn't had to. I honestly felt loved by them. It wasn't like with my mom, but it was growing into something pretty special at a good clip.

Now, my future stretched out in front of me, and it was mine to do with as I chose. I had a strange urge to skip, whistle, and twirl around with a lightness I'd not had in many years. Since I was twelve, maybe?

I thought of Nick then. His smile, and his offer of friendship, and maybe more. An almost giddy sensation rippled through me. I finally allowed myself hope that my life could be a happy one. It was up to me to allow it.

As I parked the car, I noticed my two Bertrand sisters standing in front of the soap store. They turned as soon as I got out and shut my door. Both waved and grinned. They were a part of me. We were a blend of each other.

Leah stepped up and hugged me first. "Carly filled me in on your idea about opening a business. I can totally see it, Allison. You're so creative and talented. Lydia sings your praises to anyone who will listen. I can't think of a better way to use that talent than doing what you do best."

"Thanks so much. This is something I've finally allowed myself to think about in real terms. My mind has been working overtime on the details." In fact, I could actually see the store as I intended it to be when I closed my eyes.

I still had the keys from Mrs. Sibley, so I opened the front door and got a sudden rush of excitement over having my sisters here with me.

"This is such a great space, Allison. What kind of shop do you envision? I mean, what type of products?" Leah asked.

"I've thought about selling soaps and candles as gift items, same as the previous owners. I would love to stock eclectic art pieces, floral arrangements, and old books. Basically, anything that makes a home special besides the furniture. Well, maybe some small tables, shelves, and definitely lamps and a few fixtures.

"Wow, sounds like you can see it clearly in your mind," Carly said. "I don't think there's anything like what you've described here in town."

"Lydia and I discussed doing some wholesale and retail and maybe online sales. Of course, so much of it would be seasonal merchandise." I *could* see it in my mind clearly.

"Well, I'll do anything I can to help you get your venture started," Leah said. "I've got a line on some new artists who might love to have their work on consignment."

"That would be awesome, Leah."

I pointed to different areas and described my vision to my enthusiastic sisters. They shared a few thoughts as to some things I might consider. All in all, having them share this with me felt like something out of a feel-good movie where everything turned rosy in the end. I had hope now.

AFTER LEAH AND Carly left, I made up my mind to see Nick. Instead of texting, I decided to stop by his house and surprise him, if I could catch him at home. I needed to have this conversation with him.

Mrs. Landry was out in her yard pulling weeds and dressed in a sun hat and jeans. "Oh, hi. Is Nick home?" I didn't see his truck, but I also couldn't see the entire driveway, as it curved around to the side.

"Oh, hello, Allison. Nick's upstairs at his place. But I wondered if you would like to have a cup of coffee with me first?"

I didn't want to. I wanted to see Nick right then. But there was something in the woman's tone that demanded I give her what she'd asked for.

"Okay. I guess I could spare a few minutes."

"Lovely. Come on inside and let's chat."

Mrs. Landry was a spotless housekeeper and a marvelous hostess. I wondered if this was the norm around here or if she was exceptionally good at it. "Your home is gorgeous."

She waved away my compliment as if she was swatting at

an unseen gnat. "Thank you, dear." Mrs. Landry waited a beat and then said, "Did you know that Nick's father is half Creole?"

I had no idea how to respond to that. I mean, I figured he was at least part Creole, but I honestly hadn't given it much thought besides the day I'd met him. And that was only because I was interested in the local cultures. "I believe Nick mentioned it once."

"How do you feel about that?" the woman asked, staring at me, a shrewd expression in her eyes.

"I like Nick, and his being Creole isn't something that I have a strong opinion on. It's a part of who he is." I wanted to ask if it bothered her.

"Well, you know some folks around here *do* discriminate against Creole people. I just wanted you to know in case you weren't sure. And Nick has borne the brunt of discrimination by some of the women he's dated."

"That's awful. I'm sorry to hear it."

"You do understand that we have some pretty high standards, do you not?"

Again, I measured my response at her haughty statement, or was it a question? Was I supposed to bow or kiss her ring? "Okay."

"I mean that not just anybody is right for our son."

A man walked into the room then. "Stella, what are you telling this poor girl?" He grinned at me with the same breathtaking smile as his son. They looked so much alike in that moment, I was stunned. "Hi there, I'm Bud Landry, short for Broderick."

I shook the hand he offered. "It's nice to meet you, Mr.

Landry."

"Nope. Just Bud. I'm Bud to everybody." He glanced over at his wife. "Are you trying to scare her off, Stella? I heard that last crack about our *standards*."

Stella appeared to flush with embarrassment. "I-I just wanted Allison to know that she's special because Nick likes her."

Her explanation made little sense, and Bud shook his head and rolled his eyes. "We're not so fancy. Nick's her baby and she wants to protect his heart."

His explanation made more sense. "I'm not offended. I imagine if I ever had a child, I'd be equally protective."

"Of course I meant no offense. You know Nick's dying to have children, right?"

"We haven't discussed it." I took a sip of my coffee, looking away. *Children.* I hadn't even gotten that far in my mind when it came to Nick.

"How old are you, Allison?" she asked.

"That's enough, Stella." Bud skewered his wife with a glare and then turned to me with a friendlier expression. "Nick's home. You can go on up if you'd like."

Snatching the excuse to get the heck out of there, I thanked Stella Landry for her hospitality. She smiled in a rather coy way. I figured she'd achieved her goal.

Children. I'd always wanted one or two but figured that wasn't in my life's plan since I didn't have a father for them. The idea that Nick felt so strongly about having a family slowed my roll. It was something I hadn't considered. I didn't even know if I could have a child. I was thirty-five already, and the idea was overwhelming.

And then there were the strong drugs I'd taken for my cancer treatment. I'd not had my fertility checked afterward. I'd had no reason to thus far.

Nick opened the door, his hair a little disheveled. He looked super sexy, and I wanted to throw myself in his arms. Now that I'd made the decision to make Cypress Bayou my home, I couldn't wait to share the good news. Except now I wasn't so sure. Because of the way his mother had made her suggestions about Nick's strong desire for children.

"Oh, hey. What a surprise. Come on in." He mirrored his dad's smile. "Can I get you anything?"

I shook my head and sat down on the sofa. Nick sat down beside me. "I would've been here a little sooner except your mom invited me in for a cup of coffee almost before I was out of the car."

"What did she say?" His expression became guarded.

I knew what I had to do then. "I'm planning to stay here in Cypress Bayou permanently. But I'm not sure about where we go from here."

"What do mean?" He recoiled as if I'd slapped him, his expression stunned.

"Because it isn't what's in your best interest. *I'm* not in your best interest." My throat clogged saying the words. "Or, maybe I'm not." My mind was a jumble.

"You'll need to explain that a little better so that I can understand why you're saying this."

"I'd hate for either one of us to get hurt." By his expression, I could tell he was already hurt by my words.

"You're still not making this clear. I don't understand." He was frowning hard at me now. "I thought you liked me."

"I did—do." And now I knew what I wanted, but could I give him what he wanted most?

"Why can't we let this play out and see what happens?"

Oh, how I wanted to do exactly that, but it wasn't right for me to deprive him of his life's dream. "I—need to see about some things." I looked into his troubled gaze and felt my heart squeeze. "I need to go now." I stood, needing to bolt.

He stood too, continuing to stare into my eyes. "I don't know what's happening here, Allison, but whatever this is, I don't want to stop seeing you unless you don't care about me like I do you."

"I've got—things." He let me out and I nearly sprinted to my car, feeling ridiculous about my behavior. I hadn't made it clear why I was pulling back from him, and I felt terrible about that. My fear of his eventually rejecting me over my questionable fertility was overwhelming now.

I drove the short distance to my apartment, wiping tears from my eyes. Truth was, I liked Nick. Probably more than I'd ever liked any guy. Well, I might even love him. *Did I love him?*

I tried to slow my breathing down by sitting in my car and staring at the Christmas lights around me. Nick had been such a special friend since I'd been here. No, he'd been more than a friend from the very first day I'd arrived. I'd put him in the friend zone most days because it was easier than figuring out what we were to each other. No lines had been crossed into romance. No kissing or touching, but the few times he'd taken my hand or slipped an arm around my shoulders had been magical.

I'd been avoiding anything more with Nick because it meant I didn't have to face my indecision about Cypress Bayou and trying to fit in with the Bertrands. But if I was honest, the idea of not seeing Nick was heartbreaking.

CHAPTER TWENTY-FIVE

THE ANSWER BECAME pretty clear after only a few minutes' deliberation as to what was happening with Allison. His mother. She'd done what she always did, which was to try and fix things for him. She'd done it throughout school and whenever she believed he'd been slighted or treated unfairly.

As an only child growing up, it was his main source of contention with her. Nick tried to understand and believe his best interests were being considered, but the interference was maddening mostly. And it didn't seem to matter how many times he told her to butt out.

She'd gone too far this time. He didn't know what she'd said to Allison, but it must have been a doozie.

Nick didn't often yell at his own mother, but boy did she deserve it sometimes. He pulled on his shoes and headed toward the house. He didn't knock. Just strode right in and found her in the kitchen.

"Oh, hi, honey. You still hungry?" Her expression was pure innocence as she loaded the dishwasher.

"Mom, what did you say to Allison?"

"Oh, not much. We just had a nice chat is all. I do like to get to know the people you spend your time with."

"She left your house then came over and told me we

shouldn't see each other."

She put her hand over her heart in a dramatic gesture. "Oh, I'm so sorry, Nick."

"But you're not sorry, are you?" He narrowed his eyes, seeing beyond that feigned innocence. "Tell me now."

"Very well. I think she's a nice girl, but not the right one for you. I *know* you, son, and I know she couldn't have made you happy."

"Why do you think that?"

"Because you want children and she's had all those cancer drugs pumped into her system. I've heard how they can affect a woman's fertility—especially women of a certain age." She lifted her brows in a "you know what I mean" expression.

Nick was outraged on Allison's behalf. "She's not too old to have children or start a family, and we haven't discussed it yet. I asked you to let me handle my relationships, Mom. I'm not some little boy who needs his mommy to protect him from scraped knees or a bully."

"I think you should give it some thought, dear, before you go rushing back to her. Think about your goals. Say the two of you dated for a year, got married, and then started trying to have a family. What if she's infertile? What then? Are you ready to give up on your dreams of a family?"

He wanted to yell at her. To tell her she was wrong. Maybe she wasn't even wrong about the fertility issue, but she was wrong to interfere in his life like that. "Allison's fertility is her business."

"Well, you know I worry." She shrugged it off as if she'd ordered her dad the wrong sandwich or something equally unimportant.

He stood and stared at his mother, clenching his jaw. "Don't ever do that again." It wasn't the first time he'd said this to her, but it was the last time he would allow her to meddle. This time it mattered in a big way.

She started to say something, and he held up his hand. "Just don't." He turned and left his parents' house, a sick feeling in his gut.

I'D DONE THE right thing, I knew it. Nick was such a great guy that he'd never break up with me because I couldn't give him all the kids he clearly wanted. There was no way I would make him live with regret.

As I worked on orders at Nana's kitchen table, I played Christmas music and enjoyed the nice breeze through the open windows. The physical therapist had come today and was pleased with Nana's rapid progress. Nana was thrilled to be back in her home and ready to be about her regular busy schedule, though she'd only been out of the hospital for a few days. I would go back to my apartment soon but would miss her company. Nana was taking her nap at the moment and then we would have lunch together.

Normally, I liked going into the shop, but I didn't feel very social today. I was wallowing just a little. I'd enjoyed working from Nana's house and didn't see any real reason to head back into town today.

Nana came into the kitchen with the help of her walker. "Hi, darling. How's it going in here?"

"It's good. I'm about to today's halfway mark, so I can stop for lunch."

"I know how much Lydia appreciates your work. And please thank her for allowing you to work here so you can babysit me."

"So far, it's worked out pretty well."

"I can tell you're moping a little. Care to tell me about it?"

Tears rushed to my eyes unexpectedly at her kind expression. "I'm okay. I'm just not sure where Nick and I are headed right now."

"Oh, honey, I'm sorry to hear it." Nana carefully sat down beside me and reached over for my hand.

"I'll be okay. It was a problem that couldn't be solved."

"In my experience, there are very few problems that can't be solved."

"Am I too old to start a family?" I said it and sighed. "And what if I'm infertile after the chemo?"

"What? You're never too old for that, Allison. It sounds like these are questions that can be answered with a few tests. Just because you're getting a later start, doesn't mean you can't have children, even if, for some reason you couldn't bear any."

"Mrs. Landry pointed out that Nick has always wanted children, as in more than one."

Nana's expression changed into one I'd never seen. Angry. "That Stella Landry is a real piece of work is what she is. How dare she try and sabotage things between you and Nick. I've a mind to tell her what's what."

"No. It's okay. She was right to tell me because so far,

Nick hasn't."

"She's done this to poor Nick since he was a teen. Nobody is ever good enough for her little boy. We're lucky he didn't turn out to be a spoiled brat. He's got enough of Bud Landry in him to offset Stella, thankfully."

"Yes, Mr. Landry seemed nice."

"Well, I'm getting a little hungry. How about you?" She changed the subject then, and I was grateful.

We made lunch together since I couldn't seem to shoo Nana from the kitchen.

THE OUTSIDE OF Leah and Jake's new home was completely decked out for Christmas. There were multi-colored lights outside and on the trees. The landscaping was new, so the fledgling shrubs likely wouldn't bear the weight of hot lights. But it all looked marvelous. I couldn't wait to see inside.

Leah opened the door right on cue as I pushed the doorbell. "Hi there, Allison. I'm so glad we could get together at the last minute." Karen was on Nana duty, so she wouldn't be joining them today.

"Sure. The house looks festive." I noticed she'd put up a fresh tree in the living room chock-full of ornaments, bows, poinsettias, and bright white lights.

She'd invited us over to discuss the plan for Christmas Festival and a casual dinner.

"Wow. This all looks great."

"I decided to go all out this year since we're finally in our house instead of the apartment. Last year, we decorated over there, but not like this."

"Yes, I'm still working on getting things ready for the party. Lydia loaned me some garland and other decorations she had in her storeroom."

Carly entered the kitchen where they were setting the table. We nodded to each other and smiled. "So, Allison, tell us what you plan for the open house?" We'd had a few conversations regarding food and such already.

"The food will be delivered Thursday evening before the open house. I had it catered from the café down the block. I made sure it's all finger food, and nothing too messy. And no red wine. I know people aren't nearly as careful during parties as they would be in their own homes."

LEAH NODDED. "EVERY year somebody makes a big mess or breaks something during the open house, so don't get upset over stains and spills. Certainly not on our account. Plus, we're opening it up to the public, so take a deep breath."

They'd all insisted on pitching in for the food and had Venmoed me their portion. "Thanks for helping out with the costs."

"Don't mention it. We do it this way every year since it gives us all a place to hang out downtown for the celebrations and fireworks."

"I guess I'd better get my tree up."

"Oh, that reminds me, can everybody head over to Nana's house and help her decorate tomorrow evening?" Everybody nodded, including me. Leah turned to me and said, "We usually do it right after Thanksgiving."

"I'm available. I'll be Christmas shopping with Elizabeth in Shreveport on Sunday, but this week, I've got some wiggle room to get things ready since I've been working from home." I enjoyed doing the work in the evenings listening to Christmas music.

"Shopping with Elizabeth? I can't even imagine it." Leah raised a brow, possibly in question of my sanity. "But that's just her and me."

"I get it. But she seems set on having some kind of relationship with me. I know that can't be easy considering she's been an only child her entire life." I would stick up for Elizabeth just like I stuck up for the Bertrands.

"She can't be *all* bad, can she?" Carly commented.

"I think she's very defensive. But you'll be glad to know she isn't hung up on Jake anymore." I was happy to share this with Leah since they'd had such a contentious relationship in the past.

"What? Who's hung up on me?" Jake entered the kitchen, followed by Tanner.

We settled in for a huge meal and lots of family laughter. I only felt a little bit sad because I was still missing Nick.

CHAPTER TWENTY-SIX

I DRESSED IN jeans and a reindeer sweatshirt to help my siblings decorate Nana's house for Christmas. Since Nick and I had decorated the storefront downstairs and my balcony, I'd decided that tomorrow I could spend the day working and the evening inside my apartment putting up a fresh Christmas tree and the few special items I'd brought with me and collected from Lydia's storeroom. That gave me a little more time to prepare for the Christmas Festival.

Right before I left for Nana's house, the buzzer sounded signaling company. I pressed the button expecting it was either a delivery or one of my many relatives. "Hello?"

"Allison, it's Nick. Can I come up?" His deep voice sent a wave of emotion through me.

"Sure. I'll be right down." I ran a hand through my still-short hair to fluff it. Right then, I was glad I'd put on makeup and was currently wearing his favorite pair of jeans.

When I reached the bottom of the stairs and opened the gate and saw him, I had the sudden urge to fall into Nick's arms. I worked to temper my joy and relief that he'd come over. I wasn't sure why he was here but seeing him thrilled me. "Oh, hi. Come in."

His face was so dear to me, and I'd missed it. "Thanks for seeing me."

"Of course. I'm leaving in a few to decorate Nana's house. What's up?" I'd let him inside the loft and gestured that he should sit.

His expression was grim, and I held my breath, worried that I might not like what he was about to say. "Allison, I needed to see you. My mom told me what she said to you about my wanting a family. That's true, but it's not any reason for us to be apart."

I stared at him but didn't speak, but I could feel my heartbeat accelerate as I absorbed his words.

"I want to be with you, Allison. We haven't known each other long, but to me it feels like a lifetime—like I knew you before. From the day we met, it was magic."

I tried to control the hope rising inside me. "But what if I can't have children? I mean, I want to more than anything, but what if I can't?"

"We will have a family if it's what you want too. I don't care how we do it."

A sparkle of joy ignited in my heart. I'd been willing to sacrifice my happiness so that Nick could have what he needed, but he was telling me that *I* was what he needed. "Are you sure? Because you shouldn't settle for anything less than your dreams."

"You are my dream come true, Allison, and I'm in love with you."

The sparkle ignited into full-blown fireworks in my chest. Tears rolled down my cheeks. Nick's gaze was honest and true. "I love you too, Nick."

He gently leaned in, and it was everything I'd hoped for in a kiss. I stepped closer and I breathed in the scent of him.

I wanted to kiss this man until we were very, very old.

I WORE MY fancy new shoes, my Christmas present from Elizabeth, on the opening day of the festival. They were wildly expensive, and I felt like a princess. But the heels were higher than I normally wore and by around five p.m. I was ready to fling them off the balcony. Half or more of the town, it seemed, had shown up at my apartment to meet me. All they'd needed was an invitation. Their welcome and acceptance was something I'd not expected. I overcame my initial shyness and found myself enjoying meeting everyone. They were friendly and curious but kind.

My entire family, besides Nana, attended the open house. Even Elizabeth showed up to support me. She and the rest of the Bertrands were cordial to one another, so that eased my mind a lot.

"Looks like you're a hit." Nick stood beside me on the balcony as I'd gone out to get some fresh air. "I knew they'd love you."

I turned to him and sighed. How could I have gotten so lucky? A month ago, I'd doubted my future here, and now I had everything to look forward to. Surrounded by family, new friends, and Christmas. It was a dream come true.

As darkness descended over the town and its many lights, fireworks lit up the sky. I don't think I'd ever seen anything more beautiful.

ON CHRISTMAS MORNING, I was barely awake when Nick texted. My head was still a little fuzzy from the red wine I'd consumed at last night's gift exchange with the Kellers. I'd agreed to do Christmas Eve with them and Christmas Day with the Bertrands.

Merry Christmas! Can I come over in thirty minutes?

My heart overflowed with love for him, and I couldn't wait to see him. We'd decided to slip in a little private time for the two of us to exchange gifts since we both had family commitments today. But I couldn't help joking around a little, so I replied: *If you'd like to see me in my pajamas unshowered.*

I'd worn a pair of red plaid flannel pajamas to bed like I'd always done on Christmas Eve. It reminded me of my past Christmases with Mom and Dad in our sweet little house in Naperville.

His reply made me laugh: *Stay just the way you are.*

I texted: *I'll brush my teeth first, okay?* To which he sent a thumbs-up and a heart emoji.

I'd barely brushed my teeth and dragged a brush through my messy hair when he arrived, but I was thrilled to see him despite my appearance and lack of caffeine. "Good morning." I greeted him barefoot downstairs instead of buzzing him up.

As we stepped inside the apartment together, the intensity of his expression told me this was our moment, the one that would step us into our future together. Our eyes held, and Nick pulled me into his arms for a lingering kiss without even a tiny bit of hesitation from me. It was only our second kiss but I'd already memorized the scent and taste of him.

"Merry Christmas, Allison."

"Merry Christmas." It was icy cold this morning, but the sun was shining. My feet were still freezing, so I grabbed my slippers and shoved them on my feet, having forgotten them because I was so excited to see Nick.

"Wow, it's cold today. Did you look outside across the bayou?" he asked.

"No, I haven't yet. I haven't even had coffee." I hadn't looked past him when he'd arrived.

He led me to the large window and pulled the curtains aside. There was about two inches of snow on the ground, which made my heart leap. "I can't believe it."

"Well, it's not real, but I wanted you to see snow on Christmas morning, like you did in Chicago, so I rented a snow machine. You'll notice that it's only in front of your apartment."

I hadn't noticed, but I was so touched by his desire to make me happy that tears flooded my eyes. "That's the sweetest thing anyone's ever done for me." I slid my arms around his waist, and he returned the embrace.

"Remind me to buy a snow machine so I can do this every year." He grinned at me, and I realized he was holding a box in his hands.

I asked the obvious. "Is that for me?"

"Why, yes, it is."

"Wait. Let me get yours." I moved toward my Christmas tree and reached for the Santa bag with Nick's name on the tag.

We sat on the sofa together as I handed him his gift. "Open yours first," I said.

He set the bag down between us and pulled out the item on top. "A scarf. It's really nice. Thanks." He wrapped the soft cashmere around his neck.

"There's something else there," I said, excited about his reaction. The scarf had been an afterthought.

Nick reached back into the bag and pulled out a silver picture frame. In it, I'd placed a photo that Leah had taken of us the night of my welcoming dinner. I was amazed at how tender and purely smitten our expressions were as we gazed at one another. When I'd seen it the first time, I knew I wanted to share it with Nick.

He looked up at me with his heart in his eyes. "It's so obvious how we felt, even that first night. Thank you for this. I'll treasure it, Allison." He leaned forward and kissed my lips gently.

I looked down at the tiny box in my lap, nervous about what it was.

"Go ahead, open it."

I carefully unwrapped the box and lifted the tiny lid. It was a delicate silver chain with a filigree snowflake—the most beautiful thing I'd ever seen.

"Oh, it's perfect, Nick."

"Here, put it on." He lifted the dainty pendant from its red velvet bed, and I turned around so he could fasten it. "There. The snowflake is to symbolize our first Christmas together."

"Nick, I'm so happy." His heart was tender and sweet.

"Me too, my love."

EPILOGUE

A year later

"OUR GUESTS WILL be arriving soon." Nick nuzzled my ear as I tied a sparkly bow onto the small, flocked tree. We were hosting our Christmas Festival open house in my new shop, which promised to be an annual event. The air was cold and crisp, and everywhere we went there was proof of Christmas. We even had the possibility of snow in the forecast.

"Yes. I'm done." I put away my hot glue gun and washed my hands. My shop was a dream come true. Sure, it had taken a lot of hard work and lost sleep to get started, but business was already steady, even before the holidays. I'd contacted the soap makers who'd been here before and asked if I could sell their stock, which made the people here in town very happy. Now, I ordered regularly from them. I had candles in stock, wreaths, and every kind of holiday décor. From Halloween to Christmas season, it was all Christmas all the time.

After Christmas, I would go back to selling home accessories and gifts that weren't holiday themed. Mrs. Sibley and I had struck up a deal for a combined rent of the loft and the retail space, and she'd given me a fantastic offer.

Nana had recovered almost fully from her stroke, and she

and Karen both helped out in my store. They'd all insisted on helping. Even Elizabeth stopped in regularly. I still wasn't especially close with the judge, but we were getting to know each other. He'd been taken off the bench permanently but hadn't gone to prison. He was on probation for the foreseeable future, so he'd gotten what was coming to him—pretty much.

Carson, Tanner and Jake's dad had had the book thrown at him. He wouldn't see the outside of prison in his lifetime, which suited pretty much everyone, even his sons. The man was pure evil, and he'd finally pay his debt to the town.

Leah and Carly were both pregnant, which was such a hoot because so was I. Our children would know such love and kinship with their cousins, something I'd never had. Nick and I had decided to get married almost immediately after Christmas last year because we were eager to start a family. I hadn't wanted a big wedding, so we'd decided on a small ceremony with family at Nana's house. Karen wasn't happy about that.

I'd gotten pregnant almost immediately, much to our delight and surprise. "Oh, that was a big one." I looked down to my very pregnant belly and imagined the little human inside as she kicked again. I was due in three weeks and Nick was very protective of us both.

To me, Christmas was every day.

The End

Want more? Check out Carly and Tanner's story in *Secrets in Cypress Bayou*!

Join Tule Publishing's newsletter for more great reads and weekly deals!

If you enjoyed *A Bayou Christmas*,
you'll love the other books in the...

Louisiana series

Book 1: *Home to Cypress Bayou*

Book 2: *Secrets in Cypress Bayou*

Book 3: *A Bayou Christmas*

Available now at your favorite online retailer!

More Books by Susan Sands
The Alabama series

Book 1: *Again, Alabama*

Book 2: *Love, Alabama*

Book 3: *Forever, Alabama*

Book 4: *Christmas, Alabama*

Book 5: *Noel, Alabama*

Available now at your favorite online retailer!

About the Author

Susan Sands grew up in a real life Southern Footloose town, complete with her senior class hosting the first ever prom in the history of their tiny public school. Is it any wonder she writes Southern small town stories full of porch swings, fun and romance?

Susan lives in suburban Atlanta surrounded by her husband, three young adult kiddos and lots of material for her next book.

Thank you for reading

A Bayou Christmas

If you enjoyed this book, you can find more from all our great authors at TulePublishing.com, or from your favorite online retailer.

CPSIA information can be obtained
at www.ICGtesting.com
Printed in the USA
BVHW090032291022
650563BV00003B/538